In Whispers

Also by Thomas Peacock
(as author or co-author)

The Forever Sky
Collected Wisdom: American Indian Education
Ojibwe Waasa Inaabidaa/We Look in All Directions
The Good Path
The Seventh Generation
The Four Hills of Life: Ojibwe Wisdom
To Be Free: Understanding and Eliminating Racism
The Tao of Nookomis
Beginnings: The Homeward Journey of Donovan Manypenny
The Forever Sky
The Fire
The Dancers
The Wolf's Trail
Walking Softly

In Whispers

Simon and Carolina

Thomas D. Peacock

Dovetailed Press LLC

The Medicine Dance (for Becca)

Sometimes at night
when sleep takes me to that place
where all things are possible
and the earth and sky merge as one
I dream

and tonight, in a dream
I hear the voices of old men
long passed on to the spirit world
gathered there among the sky spirits
within the circle of the wolf's trail
and the path of souls and night sun
there
singing
their voices high and in the familiar sing-song
of the old time Ojibwe

there around the drum
their voices
echoing off the big water
and sky filled with stars
too many to even wonder

singing, singing

then, in the forever sky
my beautiful daughter
there
her hair and dark eyes
there in her jingle dress
she dances, head held high
proud

dancing, dancing

Contents

Preface

Disguised as educational institutions, Indian boarding schools furthered the government's goals to dispossess Indigenous people from their land, assimilate hundreds of thousands of Indian children into non-Native culture, and erase their Indigenous identities. The boarding schools often prohibited Indian children from speaking their languages and banned them from practicing their cultures and traditions.

Many children did not survive this era and many of the children who returned to their communities had endured significant abuse. The effects of this era continue to live in Indian boarding school survivors and their descendants, and Indigenous communities continue to feel the effects through various forms of trauma. However, despite the abuse and trauma caused by this era, Indian boarding school survivors exhibited resiliency techniques that remain part of Indigenous communities today.[1]

Part One

CHAPTER ONE

Vince Gill

Dreammaker

> I dream of you often
> when the deep blue night horses run in me
> you, the maker of dreams
> and maker of feathers and wings
> I see you through my childhood eyes
> you sing to me softly through darkness lit
> by kerosene lamps and love
>
> your songs were lightening over the hills
> you are missed like rain
>
> it's been years now and only the dreams
>
> I do not wish to awaken from this dream
> I do not wish to awaken from this dream

Simon

This was all a long time ago.

Sometimes, in late evenings when I am too restless to sleep and memory runs deep in me, I imagine you come and sit beside me. And when it happens, reality blurs and I am transported back to that time and place when we were young again.

There we were, sitting behind the girls' dorm of the sister school in a field of wildflowers and sage and red clover. You in a faded cotton dress and oversized black-laced boots. There, your dark eyes, hair and skin. There, that first awkward kiss, when I turned my head away, thinking it would be on the cheek, but instead your hand touching my face and turning me to meet your lips.

There, where we dreamed.

You, just fourteen years old. I can feel the warmth of your body next to mine.

"Simon." Your voice. Soft. In a whisper, the way we spoke to each other back then, so the matrons and nuns at the sister school couldn't hear us speaking in the language. Back when we were hiding from the priest.

"Take my hand. *Daga* please," you said.

So, I opened my old hand, rough and scarred from many years of hard work and hard living, and took your hand in mine.

And then, suddenly, I am thirteen years old again.

My voice breaks, speaks of too many winters alone.

"I've missed you," I say.

And then I feel your head rest on my shoulder.

"Where have you been?" I ask. Again.

In a whisper.

"Where have you been?"

My life. I was born Simon Pendagayosh in the year 1944 to Susan and Benjamin Pendagayosh in *Nagachiwanong*, on a hill overlooking the river that flows through the Fond du Lac Reservation in Northern Minnesota. Born in a tarpaper shack built with scraps of lumber and tarpaper and bent nails scavenged from the wood mill dump down the hill. Born into a family of thirteen children in the bush. Born in high winter on the coldest day of the year, born of woodsmoke and rabbit stew and bear grease. Brought into this world by an old auntie who knew no English, chewed snuff and smoked a pipe and had no teeth.

My father worked as a logger for a timber baron whose crews were clear-cutting sections of reservation land that stretched for miles across the horizon. He and my uncles and their cousins spent long days in the bush upriver. Hard, dangerous work, using bow saws and axes. They would drag themselves home each day, exhausted, back up the hill, smelling of sweat and pine and chew. I remember them now, walking the trail from the village up the railroad tracks to work, swinging their black, metal lunch pails as they went along, all the while speaking in the language. Six days a week, ten hours a day.

My mother got up early on father's work days before first light to pack his lunch, sometimes bacon grease slathered on thick, home-made bread, sprinkled with sugar, or lug (lugalate, a pan bread made with flour and baking soda) and lard wrapped in wax paper, a jug of tea. When the hunt was good there was venison or rabbit. I remember them together, early in the morning at first light, thinking us kids were still asleep, talking soft and low in the language, back and forth, their voices mingled with the sounds of bacon frying, the shuffling of feet across the kitchen floor, and smell of the wood stove.

On Sundays when my father wasn't working, he'd clean up good and slick his hair back with bear grease, and my mother would put on a clean dress and us kids would put on our Sunday go to church clothes and we would walk the dirt road that led up to the church a mile or so to worship at the Catholic mission.

My mother sang in the choir. My father sat with the men from the village in the back pews. Kids sat in front with all the sinners, at least that's what my mother would say.

"You sinners need to sit close and listen to them words," she'd say to us mischievously.

Then she would smile and point a long, brown, skinny finger right between my eyes and motion with her lips for me to join all the other young, mostly boys, sinners up in the front pew.

Always I dream of those times. The colors, smells, voices.

After church we'd gather outside for visiting, my mother with the women and father with the men, the girls with each other, and us village boys.

We'd talk. All in the language. That's all we talked then.

Years later when I was homeless and living on the streets in Minneapolis, I made my way past a church one holiday season. They were singing Silent Night and it took me years back, up to that little reservation church where all the village women would sing it as well, but in the language. And I remember the way it was sung like it was yesterday, sad and low and in the sing-song of our beautiful, beautiful language.

And then I sang it too as I walked along that Christmas Eve, low and mournful and under my breath as I walked down Franklin Avenue to the only shelter that would take me that night.

That silent night.

> *Gichitwaa-dibikad*
> *waaseyaaziwin maa*
> *ayaamagad ayaad Mary*
> *baanizid Abinoojii niigid*
> *Christ sa gii-niigid*
> *Gichitwaa-dibikad*
> *gichi-zegiziwag*
> *apii wayaabandamowaad*
> *i'iw bishigendaagoziwin*

Christ sa gii-niigid
Gichitwaa-dibikad
Gizhemanidoo sa
gichi-bishigendaagozi
miigiwed iniw Ogwisan
Jesus gii-niigid[2]

My brothers and sisters. Some of them gone now. One, drunk driving through trees and telephone poles. Another turning a .22 pistol to their head. One losing toes and feet and fingers to diabetes. Some doing fine though, living the good life. Upstanding rez folk, tribal bureaucrats, would be tribal politicians. One sister married a white man and lives in a fancy house in town. Of those living, most I haven't seen in years. The last time I saw them together at the same time, I was drunk, having hitchhiked north to our mother's funeral, swaying back and forth at the gravesite as one of her sisters, my auntie, was singing How Great Thou Art, and I, thinking aloud, how any great and merciful god could do this and all the other horrific things that have been done to us, to our people.

And still the people of my village, and those in my family still walking *aki*, earth, led by Auntie, all with heads bowed, singing,

NiManidoom, maamakaadeniminaan
gakina akiiwan ozhitooyan
anangoog gaye aanakwad chi-madweweg
gimashkawiziiwin minz'we ayaag

Nanagamoomagad sa go ninde'
Gwetaamigwendaagoziyan
nanagamoomagad sa go ninde'
Gechi-ishpendaagoziyan!

Megwekwaang gechi-bishigendaagwak,
bineshiijyag mino' amaazowaad,
wajiwing gichi-minwaabishinaan
zhiibiiwishe chi-minwewejiwang
Mikwendamaan Manidoo gii-miigiwed
Ogwisan maa aazhideyaatigong
bimoondang gakina baataaziwinan
ina'amaan Gwetaamigoziyan
Apii go Christ ninga-bi-gaganoonig
giiwewizhid ninga-moojigendam
ojijiingwanigaabawiitawag sa
nagamoyaan gechi-ishpenimag[3]

Later, my sister Annie, the one married to the white man, slipped me a few bucks and bought me a bus ticket back to the Cities, brother Johnny a pint of Five Star Brandy, the good stuff. I, sitting in the back of the bus as it roared on down the highway, singing, until the driver hollered back for me to shut the hell up.

How great thou art
Yah ay hei ah
How great thou art
Yah ay hei ah

Once my mother and father passed my sister Annie and brother Johnny were the only siblings who tried to keep in touch with me, if they could find me. And at least when I was sober, I'd try to keep in touch with them. I'd send them some of my poems.

"I'm working on this poem," I'd say. "It needs some work but I like where it's going."

Johnny would always write back and tell me it was "real goot," in reservation English, or say "howah." Sister wrote long letters, pages, filling me in on family matters, what everyone was up to.

She'd always end the letters with something like, "Brother, come home. Come home, we miss you. We worry about you, brother. We wonder if you are dead or alive sometimes."

And if I was sober at the time, I'd send her a note back telling her I would, someday.

"I will," I'd write. "Don't worry about me, Sister. I'm doing okay."

But we both knew full well I wasn't okay.

It was hard for them to keep in touch when I was careening in and out of benders all those years. Sometimes it would be a year or more between letters, and it would be up to me to initiate communications once I sobered up and had an address, always temporary it seemed.

Eventually, she hopped a bus to the Cities to visit me. I often wondered what that paleface husband of hers thought of his headstrong, independent Native wife. I'd sobered up for a while and she gave me a week's notice of her visit. She mentioned she wanted me to come north and be with family. I met her at the bus station downtown and gave her the grand tour of my haunts. We went to the Indian Center to meet some of the people I had become acquainted with during my sober streaks. She took me out for meals at decent restaurants. And I invited her to lunch one day as well.

"On me," I said, a sly smile on my face.

We had a meal at a feeding center at one of the churches off Cedar Avenue.

"Welcome to my world," I said when we walked in the door, all the street men staring at my sister, who looked obviously out of place there dressed in the fancy clothes she bought at the S & L Store in the town of Cloquet where she lived.

She stayed at the Andrews Hotel downtown for a couple of nights. Then I took her to the depot and put her on the bus back north. Over the years she would try to make an annual trip down, and I always looked forward to it. We enjoyed walking the city, the sanitized, safe parts, certainly not the areas I usually frequented.

And always before she left, she would ask me to make the journey home with her.

"Come home, Brother. We miss you there. Johnny said you could stay at his place until you get settled."

I always promised I would, of course, but I never did.

My brother Johnny made a similar journey one time on the Greyhound Lines and found me within hours. I was drunk, hanging out in one of the Indian bars. I got him started and we spent three, four days drinking up a storm until he was dirt broke and sleeping who knows where. On day four he woke up with a massive hangover and I felt sorry for his ass and walked him downtown to the bus depot and bid him a fond adieu.

I remember he turned to me as he was climbing into the bus.

"Take care of yourself, Brother. Keep sending your writing. Take care of yourself."

That was the last time I saw him. When I finally sobered up, months later, and wrote Sister from a shelter, she sent me a reply that Johnny had passed. Complications from diabetes, she said. We missed you there, she said. Come home, brother, she said.

I was sitting on a cot at a shelter in the Phillips neighborhood when I read her letter. I saw him in memories then. We are playing a game of lacrosse with our brothers and cousins through the open fields near our home, our parents, aunties, uncles, and grandparents all watching and cheering us on.

I remember he was good at it. Me, not so much.

In another memory, we were running through the woods behind our house when we were little boys, he and my other brothers playing war.

I, thinking, sitting on the edge of a cot at a shelter shared with others of my kind. Thinking, this is so much worse than war. This life, there are no winners here.

This life.

Sometimes I think it's memories that kept me going, alive. And I think that being sober on occasion allowed the fog to lift a bit in my brain so I could have clear thoughts.

I stayed sober for a while after hearing the news about Johnny. Normally, I suppose, hearing something like that would have sent me off on a mean one, bender, but for some reason I stayed straight.

Several days after hearing news of my brother I was walking by Little Earth housing project. Just off Cedar Avenue, and on the community bulletin board there was an announcement about a lacrosse, *baaga'adowewin*, stick making class. The game has been making a comeback in Indian country as we see a slow return to our traditions, especially among young people. I have memories of my father teaching us boys to play lacrosse, the Creator's game, he called it. A long time ago, he had said, when the different villages got together the men and boys would have very rough, competitive games of lacrosse through the woods and swamps that surrounded our village. The game, he said, went on all day, and for miles. Scoring was rare.

"Long ago," he had said, "we sometimes even played the game with our enemies. It was a substitute for warring."

So, a few days later I went to the first class there in Little Earth. The instructor was some Oneida from the Green Bay area. Lacrosse has always been big among the Iroquois people, I understand, and he reiterated it at the beginning of the class. Then he talked about the origins of the game among his people. The game was a social event and sometimes played to settle disputes. Lacrosse, he said, began among the Haudenosaunee, or Iroquois people, in what now is New York and parts of Canada.

There was another Ojibwe guy sitting by me at the back table and we spoke back and forth in the language, laughing every once in while that at one time, many generations ago, the Haudenosaunee were our mortal enemies. And now, centuries later, to have found ourselves learning the craft of stick making from one of them.

Since there are no hickory in our region, and he didn't have access to oak, the instructor brought wood from the ash tree. It's the lightest and weakest of the woods the sticks can be made of, but it's still durable enough. Each piece was about six feet long, straight grained, about an inch and a half thick.

I remember we used a planer to trim the boards down to about an inch or so. By the time we were done trimming our wood was about an inch by inch and six feet long.

He had a jig he'd made and we steamed the tongue, the hoop end, in a large pot of boiling water, and bent it in a circle. He had a form we put each hoop in once it was in a circle so it would keep the shape. Throughout the process he told us stories and we shared our own with him. I got to talk about the lacrosse we played when I was young back up on the rez.

The class went for a couple of evenings. We did more cutting and sanding and rounding off the sharp edges, put notches in the hoop to secure the leather we used for cording, drilled the holes, seven he said for the lacing. We cut the stick down to about 42 inches, sanded like mad, then added our own personal touches to it. I carved my brother's name, "Johnny," on the side of mine. Then we rubbed it with linseed oil and netted the hoop once it was dry.

I tied a couple of pigeon feathers I'd found on the street to the end of the stick to fancy it up. When I was sober I usually had pretty steady work doing day labor so I had a few extra bucks to spend. I wrapped the stick up in bubble wrap, shipping paper and nearly a whole roll of shipping tape and mailed it off to Sister with a note.

"Take this up Rez road," I said, "up there to the cemetery where they put Johnny, and set it on his grave. I think he'd appreciate it."

Another time I was walking down Franklin Avenue in the dead of winter, the snow on the sidewalk crunching beneath my feet, making a beeline for a free meal at the Minneapolis Indian Center. They were celebrating something or other, and had posted a meal for the community on their billboard. And I just couldn't pass on a free meal, especially since they were going to have fry bread and wild rice and chicken ala something.

It was cold, crisp, and clear I remember, a full moon. My breath. The only sound except for a few cars going by. A memory, I thought of my father then. His voice low and in the singsong of the old time Ojibwe first language speakers.

"It's your turn to feed the dogs," he had said to me, pointing with his lips toward the door. I imagined him then, the way the pursing of his lips and their pointing seemed to open and close the door and follow the trail down through the snow to the dog pen.

My mother had a pail of the day's scraps by the door waiting for me, some oatmeal, boiled potatoes, macaroni, bread crusts, and strips of gristle and deer bone from the fall hunt. To that my father had added a frozen cottontail rabbit, cut into three sections, fur and all, its frozen, blank, sparkling eyes staring up at me.

"Give Jake the head," he said to me. Jake was his favorite. The lead dog. An orange and white female Siberian. I remember asking him once why he gave the female a male name. He said when it was a pup, he said a bunch of names aloud to it. Janie, Jamie, Jill, Joanie. No reaction from the pup.

"How about Jake 'den?" he asked the dog, and it waddled over to him, licking his hand.

So that's how Jake became Jake. All names, you see, come with a story.

I remember taking the pail in my hand, stepping out into the cold, crisp winter air. The vapor of my breath curling up above and around me. Grandmother moon shining through the branches of the trees above. Normally I would have needed a flashlight to light the way down the path to the pen, but that night I could have nearly read in the moonlight.

The dogs knew it was suppertime. Barking, howling, jumping, butts and tails shaking madly in anticipation. I ladled their meal out into three spots in the snow and hay that formed the bed of the pen.

Jake loved the rabbit head. Half barking, half howling in delight.

Their meals nearly gone in seconds, except for the rabbit. Each took their share of it and went off in different corners to feast, lovingly removing all the meat from the bones, then grinding the bones to get at the marrow.

Before I went back to the warmth of home, I went to each of the dogs and petted them, stroking their ears, scratching deep into the thick fur of their sides and bellies, talking to each of them by name in Ojibwe and English. Even our dogs were bilingual. Jake, Asker, LaVern. Each flopping their tails loudly, lovingly, into the messy mix of snow and straw.

———✦———

I remember as I rounded a corner near the Indian center, I heard a whimper and rustling coming from a back alley, so I stopped and made my way down to a pile of garbage bags and cardboard outside a dumpster.

That's when I found her.

A soft bundle of fur, ears, and tail. One blue eye, one brown. A husky pup, something else mix breed, maybe lab, shepard, collie, I wasn't sure. She was cold and shivering so I wrapped her up in my coat, cuddling her close to my chest, heart.

"Hey there little *neej*, friend," I said in the slow, gentle way us humans so often use when speaking to our animal relatives. "What you doing hanging out by the dumpster all by your lonesome?"

I kept her hidden under my coat that night during the meal, only the people I shared a table with knowing all the squirming and muffled whimpering going on under my coat was my new friend. I shared the meal with her, of course, down to the pumpkin pie with whipped cream they served for dessert. We listened to an elder saying the blessing, a few speeches, some songs from a local drum group.

I had been through an extended period of having no friends. Being sober can sometimes mean being alone. I'd been sober, dry drunk for nearly three months, living alone in a rooming house, working day labor and living on day old and crushed twinkies from the Hostess factory store down the avenue a bit. If I'd been on a bender, I'd have all my drinking buddies to keep me company, to share our collective misery.

I took the pup home that night. And, of course she crapped all over the floor and I had to clean it up in the morning before stumbling half-awake out the door and down the hall to the toilet. At first, I was thinking I'd name her *Moo*, Ojibwe for poop. So, I called for her by her new, maybe name.

"*Umbe Moo*." Come here, Poop.

She just sat there looking at me like one of my crabby aunties.

I ended up just calling her "Pup" for the next couple of days. And it took her a few nights to get used to living with me, an old bachelor, Native, dry drunk. She'd whine and cry sometimes at night as she was sharing the bed with me, her voice high and lonesome for her mama.

That's why I ended up naming her Vince Gill, you see. Vince Gill sometimes sings high and sad and lonesome.

"That's okay Vince Gill," I'd whisper to her. "You and me, we're in this together. This life."

———⊱⊰———

I had dreams for her of course. I'd make a sled dog of her. I made a harness from some rope I'd bought at the Dollar Store and hooked it to a scuffed up red plastic sled I'd found next to the dumpster outside the building where I was rooming and I piled on a couple of broken bricks to get her used to pulling weight. As she grew, I added more weight. Soon enough, of course, she was pulling a sack of spuds and some boxes of hamburger helper from the grocery for me. In spring we transitioned to an abandoned wagon I found near the same dumpster I'd found the sled.

Sober now nearly ten months. Hanging in there by my fingernails most of the time. And at night with Vince Gill lying at my feet while watching TV my mind would drift off to memory.

I remembered when I was a boy, we'd run the dogs on a trail that circled deep in the woods from home out into the bush for five, six miles. Jake and the other two dogs. Jake in front setting the pace, Asker and LaVern behind, Jake keeping the gang line tight.

Quiet except for the dogs breathing and the runners of the sled as we made our way down the path, and my father's occasional commands to the dogs. The air cold, crisp. Sometimes it was snowing, the flakes melting when it hit my face. Sometimes the sun and tree shadows.

"Gee!" My father's command for Jake to turn to the right. "Haw!" for a left turn. Me sitting in the sled all bundled up to keep warm. Handmade mittens, scarf, and hat knitted by my mother. An old pair of worn out, on their second-generation Red Wing winter boots and wool socks. An old army coat we'd gotten by rifling through the clothes at the Salvation Army.

I think back then that was the closest I'd been to being in heaven. My father, the dogs, and me.

***

I don't know what triggered me to fall off the wagon. I hadn't touched a drink in nearly a year. Getting near steady day work. Vince Gill and I had become best buddies. I don't know. Just one night on my way back from work I saw the flashing sign of the liquor store and it had my name all over it.

"Simon," It whispered to me.

"Hey Simon," it said again.

I was drunk for days, months. Got booted out of my room for being loud and obnoxious and was living back on the streets with my drinking friends, sleeping, drinking under highway underpasses and in tents through late spring and into fall. When we needed food, we'd find it at food shelves and feeding centers scattered about the rugged underbelly of Minneapolis.

Me and Vince Gill. She had to put up with a lot of my crap. Me fighting other drunks, panhandling, stealing, sniffing, snorting, peeing my pants. Then one time I woke from my one hundredth black out and she was gone. I looked all over for her, everywhere. Maybe she got sick of me and my ways. Everyone else in my life seemed to, except the street people who shared the same lost togetherness, alone spaces that was our lives. Our shared misery, unspoken street comradery.

I loved my dog. She had been one of the few threads of normalcy in my life.

Sometimes I have this vivid dream where I am young again sitting in the sled as it weaves its way through the bush. My father standing on the back runners, pushing off, giving the dogs commands. Silent except for the sound of the dogs breathing and the runners of the sled in the snow. The vapor from our breathing rising into the sky like a prayer. Cold, crisp, a full moon lighting the way. My father, Jake, Asker, and LaVern.

And Vince Gill.

CHAPTER TWO

Mindamooyay

Carolina

I'm an old woman now, *mindamooyay*. That's what they call us in our language. Here at the hospital where I've been volunteering for the last few years, they call me Grandma Carolina. I get to visit with the children that are here, read to them. Everyone, especially children, needs a grandma and I enjoy being that for them when they find themselves here. It can be frightening for young ones when they are in hospital because of an accident, illness, treatment or operation of some sort.

I visit the Native people who end up here as well, and their families. I'll talk Ojibwe with the elder ones that still know the tongue, and I think it really helps them feel more welcome here, you know. Whether they are from Fond du Lac, White Earth, Bois Forte, Mille Lacs, Upper or Lower Sioux, Prairie Island, Grand Portage, Leech Lake, Red Lake, or wherever, they seem to really like speaking with another Native person while they are in hospital. I've been traveling on the powwow trail to all these communities most of my life so I know the places they are from, and many people whose acquaintances we share in common. If they are traditional Ojibwe people we talk only in the language, and sometimes when the nurses or aides come in the room to give medication or check on the patient or whatever, I'll tease them, saying that we are talking about them. We Native people like teasing others.

"What language are you speaking?" Some of them will say to me every once in a while.

"*Ojibwemowin*," I'll reply. "One of the first American languages."

Sometimes they don't get it, of course. They forget our people were here, and have been, for many thousands of years. Before Duluth, before St. Anthony's Hospital, back as far as when the last glacier was melting, when Lake Superior rose to near the top of the highest hill in what is today's city. Back before English, a European language, was the official language of this land. Back when the land was ours. Back before the land treaties that robbed us of our homes and livelihoods, back before Sand Creek and Wounded Knee and Sandy Lake and the Trail of Tears. Back before Columbus Day. Back before smallpox.

I still carry some of that ancestral anger, I guess. I try to keep it in check, but sometimes when I least expect it, it sneaks out like a little *booget*, fart, smells up the room, rears its ugly head. I'm not really angry. I just want people to know the truth, rather than the disinfected untruths they've learned in their history books, on television, or social media. We'd all be better off if we did. I've been told I'm a strong, Ojibwe woman. I hold my head high, proud. Sometimes I just speak my mind.

If the Native patients are elderly, and many of them are, they may have been sent off as little children to one of the mission or boarding schools like I was, we'll talk about that, only if they bring it up, because they may have bad memories of their time there. St. John's,

St. Benedict's, St. Mary's, Flandreau, Pipestone. Some ended up being sent to Wapheton Indian School in North Dakota.

So, if they bring it up, I'll tell them I was sent to St. Mary's Mission School near Granite Falls when I was in the seventh grade. How they talked my father and mother and me into it because they said that I would get a better education than I would get at the local school, and that every other Native family was sending their children there and that it would be good for me and all. And now I know, of course, that it really wasn't like that at all, and that just a generation or two before my time that Native children were forcibly taken from their homes and sent to them schools, and parents were told they would have their rations withheld if they didn't agree to it. And that the real purpose of those schools was to rid us of everything that was Native about us and make us good Christians.

And sometimes when we are talking about them schools, I'll ask about him, Simon Pendagayosh. My first love. If they knew or know him. Whatever became of him, where he is or was.

No one has ever been able to tell me about him, although some of the people from White Earth, Red Lake and Fond du Lac have mentioned that they know or knew of persons with that last name. He's never popped up on any of my Google searches either.

Sometimes my breath still catches when I say his name aloud, even knowing it's been nearly sixty years since those times, back to that place and time when we were young.

There.

I remember sometimes in late evenings when we would sneak out behind the girl's dorm of the sister school to a field of wildflowers and sage and red clover. There, his dark eyes, hair, and skin. There, our first awkward kiss, when he turned his head away, thinking it would be on the cheek, but instead my hand touching his face and turning him to meet my lips.

There, where we dreamed.

Me, just fourteen years old. I could feel the warmth of his body next to mine.

"Carolina." His voice. Soft. In a whisper, the way we spoke to each other back then, so the matrons and nuns at the sister school couldn't hear us speaking in the language. Back when we were hiding from the priest.

He, shy and rezzy as can be. Rezzy, that means quiet and backward in a nice way. Me, not so much.

"Take my hand. *Daga*, please," I'd say.

And then I'd rest my head on his shoulder.

Sometimes now late at night when I am unable to sleep, he will visit me in memory.

"Where have you been?" I'll ask. Again.

In a whisper.

"Where have you been?"

My life. I was born Carolina Shaugobay to Charles and Maria Shaugobay in 1943 at the Cass Lake Indian Hospital on the Leech Lake Reservation, way out in the bush on the south side of Lake Andrusia in northern Minnesota. I got my English name from my father, who did his basic training in the First Marine Division at Camp Legeune in North Carolina before they shipped him off to the war in Europe. My Ojibwe name is Anung, Star, a name dreamed by one of my aunties. My family, we lived out in what was known as the Mission area, named as such for the Mokahum Bible School, where Christian missionaries trained some of our men to minister to us. We didn't take to it well I guess, as my family was what we call traditional today. Back in the day they called us heathens. We did the ceremonies that were banned by the government back then, having to hold them far out in bush away from the missionaries, Indian agents and even some of our fellow Ojibwe who were Christians, who might turn us in.

We were a small family, just my sister June and I, and our parents. When I was little our grandmother lived with us until she passed. Grandmother Delia she was, always dressed in a long black dress with dark stockings and tall, laced black boots. She wore a white doily on her head and in my foggy memory, sat in a rocker by the wood stove, holding the Catholic rosary and muttering prayers. She was my father's mother, and always seemed to be scolding my sister and I. We called her grandmother Shaugobay. My mother always called her Mrs. Shaugobay. My father called her ma. I wonder if she felt a bit out of place in that her son and daughter in law, my father and mother, still followed the old ways of worshipping our Creator.

My father worked at a sawmill after the war, on the south side of the village of Cass Lake. The town was divided by a road, Ojibwe people on the north side, white folks on the south end. He walked to work and back home every day, three miles each way, past the bible school and down to the main highway, then through the scattering of tar paper shacks that made up the Ojibwe side of town.

Our home was built from scraps of green lumber from the mill where he worked, a three-room house with combined kitchen and living area and two small bedrooms. My sister and I shared a roll-away in our parent's room until grandmother Delia passed, then we moved into her old room. The house was heated with an old kitchen woodstove where all the cooking and baking was done. There was a water reservoir on the side of it that was always kept full for our weekly baths and washing clothes. As little girls, my sister and I would take turns bathing in an old wash tub that was usually kept hanging out in the shed when it wasn't being used for washing clothes or us. We didn't have electricity or running water. There was an outhouse out back, and before the age of Charmin we used old Sears catalogs as toilet paper. We got our water from a shared neighborhood well that I remember priming and hand pumping every other day, filling several milk cans and helping our father put them into a cart to haul home.

There was an old, tube battery radio in the living room we'd get to listen to every Friday evening. My mother liked to listen to swing. I remember her favorite song, *Chattanooga Choo Choo*. Today, I still ask for it on Alexa whenever I am missing my mother and those times. And my favorite back then was *Dear Hearts and Gentle People* by Bing Crosby. Nowadays, I tell Alexa to play that one as well. My father would always tune in to one of the local high school basketball games that were broadcast on Friday winter evenings.

My mother kept a large garden out back and raised all of the vegetables we needed for the year, carrots, peas, onions, tomatoes, radishes, potatoes, beans, cucumbers, beets, and squash. We had a raspberry patch as well. As little girls we helped pitch in during canning time. My parents harvested wild rice in early fall and they would parch and hand thresh it up in the back yard so we always had plenty of it for meals. Sister June and I got to jig it, dance the rice to separate the hulls from the rice. My dad had dug a small pit and lined it with a tarp and we'd put on our moccasins and get in there and dance it. We made syrup in the spring from the maples out in the bush behind our house for sweetener and cakes. We picked wild strawberries, blueberries, and chokecherries for jams and jellies, and hazelnuts for cookies. My mother also made clover honey. Every once in a while, my parents would make a batch of dandelion wine as well that they'd share with neighbors on New Year's Day, when we always had company call to wish us only good things for the coming year. Father harvested deer, grouse, ducks, beaver, and rabbits. He taught my sister and I to set snares for the rabbits in winter. Nowadays I still get a hunger for rabbit stew. I haven't had any in many, many years. And, we always had more than our share of fish from Lake Andrusia, which was full of walleye, still my favorite fish. Today, every time I make a walleye dinner, I'll boil up some spuds and make a pot of wild rice and bacon and have it as a feast whenever I think of when my sister and I were little girls living out in the bush with our parents.

My parents loved me. I know they did, even though they never told me as such. I still remember my father picking me up and throwing me in the air and catching me, and me riding pony on his leg. And my mother, when she would comb June's and my hair after our baths, she would always hum and sing an old song in the language, and she'd touch our faces with her hands, calloused from years of hard work, and kiss us both on the cheeks. Sometimes when she cooked, she'd add blueberry eyes to the pancakes, or a smile. Both my mother and father called my sister and me their baby girls.

We had a good life there, you know, out there. We were never in want of anything, never hungry or cold, always loved.

Now, whenever I travel north with my sister June to the Fourth of July powwow in Cass Lake, we take the drive down Mission Road to where we grew up, past the bible school and around what today is still called Mission Corner. There's nothing left of the home my sister June and I grew up in. Everything is gone, changed. Yet, there we are. We'll walk through the bushes where our garden was and to the clearing where our house once stood, and then we'll sit in the tall grass and watch as the wind blows it gently back and forth, bees moving from wildflower to wildflower to drink the sweet nectar.

And we, drinking the sweet nectar of our childhood memories. Sometimes there it seems I can still hear our mother's voice, soft and low in the language.

"How are my baby girls?"

My father, tossing me high in the air, catching me in a bear hug and holding me, laughing.

There. My sister and I.

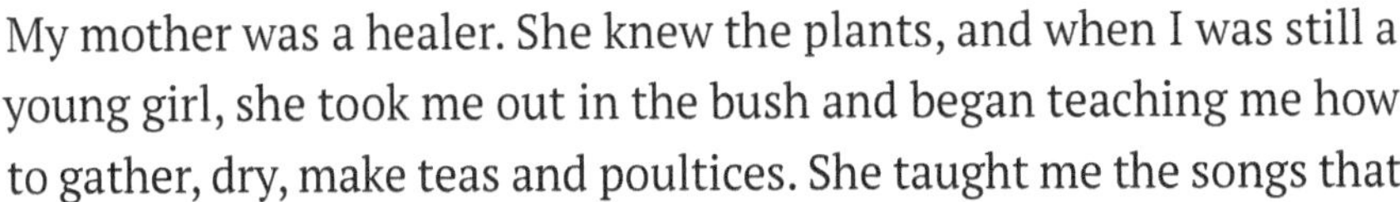

My mother was a healer. She knew the plants, and when I was still a young girl, she took me out in the bush and began teaching me how to gather, dry, make teas and poultices. She taught me the songs that are sung and prayers that are offered when gathering and making the medicines, or administering. Each song, prayer memorized. Medicinal plants aren't as effective if they aren't accompanied by prayer, or song. It's that combination of ingredients in the plants, along with those prayers and songs to our Creator that does the healing.

My sister June never showed a real interest in learning these things. She was more interested in boys and her friends. Maybe she was bit wild as well. I remember when she was a teenager, sneaking out the window at night times to meet a boy, or to go off with her friends. She'd try to drag me along as well, but I never did. It's not that I didn't want to go. I was, plain and simple, a chicken. I feared the disappointment and disapproval of our parents. June said as much every once in a while.

"Hey, *baka-aquay*, chicken," she'd say, teasingly. Then she'd make that clucking sound and flap her arms like a chicken.

She still does that on occasion nowadays, even though we are a couple of old ladies. If I'm driving too slowly or wait too long to make a turn onto a main road, or feel too guilty to taste test the grapes at the grocery store, she'll cup her hand on the side of her mouth and say, just enough so I can hear.

"*Baka-aquay.*"

That word. To this day that's what we call Kentucky Fried Chicken, KFC, "Colonel *Baka-aquay*." We've both got that rez humor down good.

Anyway, back to the plants.

The first thing my mother taught me was the four sacred medicines. We went out in the bush in the springtime and she found some red willow to gather, then we took it home and she shaved off the red bark to expose the soft white skin under it. She shaved that off, leaving the wood and core. Then she dried the shavings, and that is what we call *asemaa*, tobacco. Nowadays when we smoke it, we'll mix it half and half with Prince Albert, commercially grown.

"Tobacco is the first plant the Creator gave to us," she said. "*Asemaa* is the most important medicine. You use that, offer it, to the Creator when you gather all other plants, when you pray and sing them healing songs. Along with sage, cedar, and sweetgrass we call them the four sacred medicines. The spirits like it when we use them. These four plants are used every day and in our ceremonies. They can be used to smudge with, cleanse, offer as a blessing. Sage, cedar, and sweetgrass also have other purposes. Each plant sits at one of the four directions—tobacco the eastern door, sweetgrass the southern door, sage the west, and cedar the north."

As a young woman, I had so much to learn from my mother. Not just to be a good daughter, or a mother someday, but I willingly took on the responsibility of learning all the things to be a healer.

Sometimes in my volunteering at hospital when a patient is a traditional Native person, I'll ask them if they want me to pray and make offerings in the old way. If they consent, I'll bring out the tobacco pouch and offer them a pinch, then I'll take some for myself and I'll pray. That tobacco was given to us as a way to communicate with the spirits. It opens the doorway to the spirit world and allows our words to enter, our feelings, wishes.

Sometimes when I visit little ones, after I read to them and go back to the volunteer station, I'll take some of that tobacco out and pray silently for the young ones, you know. They are so young to be in hospital, to be suffering, and I'll ask the Creator to relieve them of their pain, or illness, that they might live long and enjoy life.

We offer that tobacco when we go out in the bush to gather the medicines. In that way the plant will know why we are there to gather it, and, in turn, it will let the other plants in the area know what we are there for, why we are gathering them. And when we seek advice from another healer, an elder, or someone who leads ceremony, we offer that tobacco. We put that sacred tobacco down before and after a fast, and when the sun comes up.

When we do ceremony, we use sage to ready the people for the teachings and the rites of the ceremony. And we use it to smudge individuals and a home to release any negative energy. We use it to cleanse sacred items like our pipes, drums, feathers, eagle bone whistles.

Sometimes when we bathe babies and young ones, we'll put some cedar in the water to cleanse. And we'll put cedar in a fire, say, at the mourning fire when a person passes, along with tobacco. Cedar crackles, and when it does it's calling the attention of the spirits to the offering that is being made. We also use cedar when we fast, and in the sweat lodge to protect everyone in there from harm. We put cedar boughs down on the floor of the sweat lodge for that, as well as the lodge used by someone who is fasting. We also make it into a healing tea, and put it in a kettle of water on the stove when we are ill and catch the healing vapors.

And lastly, sweetgrass is *ni-maama aki*, mother earth's, hair. The beautiful aroma is a reminder her gentleness, love, and kindness she shows for our people. Often when I do my healing, I'll use sweetgrass. When my mother passed, I put sweetgrass in the casket with her to remind me of her gentle love, and for all she taught me.

I gather all these four sacred medicines, and all the other plants I use for healing, and care for them. I tell people that if they have been using drugs or alcohol to avoid using, even touching, these medicines until the chemicals they are using is out of their system. I could go on and on, I suppose, describing all the plant medicines I use in healing. And I know now that I am an old woman, I need to make sure I have taught all that I know to my daughters so there will be someone to pass on that knowledge into the future.

⟶

When I was young my uncle Damien, my father's brother, was head of the lodge where we held our ceremonies. I just called him Uncle, and my father called him Brother. We went way back in the bush then, as I mentioned earlier, because our Ojibwe religion, in fact all Native religions, were illegal until the 1978 American Indian Religious Freedom Act. To think the European immigrants that first came to this land, many escaping religious persecution in Europe, once they established themselves, forbade the freedom of religion to the first people of this land. They even put it in their so-called Bill of Rights to protect that right. I guess those freedoms weren't meant for us.

Anyway, Uncle not only led ceremonies, he did namings, giving little ones their Ojibwe name, to those who would seek him out and offer tobacco and request a name. He did the *jeezikay*, the shaking tent ceremony, as well.

I remember going to my first shaking tent ceremony. The ceremony would begin at nightfall and go on for hours. People came to it if they wanted to know something, or to seek spiritual guidance, or to help with a personal issue, or if they were in pain from something, grieving maybe. There was a small, circular wigwam, like a teepee I suppose, and Uncle was inside singing and praying. The wigwam would shake. I remember there were voices coming from it, different spirits. One voice sounded like a turtle. Individuals would go up to the wigwam and Uncle would ask them to tell the spirits what they were in need of, and they would receive answers.

Sometimes when I was having an inner struggle with something I'd go up to the wigwam and ask for guidance, and the spirits would give me direction. One time after I became an adult, I thought I might ask about Simon Pendagayosh, where he was, but I didn't because I was a married woman by then and it wouldn't have been proper to do that. You would think that my memories of him would have long faded, but they didn't. He always had a place in my heart. Love, you see, knows no bounds.

Our ceremonies have been with us for a long, long time. They are nearly as old as we have been Ojibwe. We weren't always gifted with them. There is an old story of a young boy who was taken into the sky to learn teachings from seven grandfathers. It's a beautiful, necessary story that everyone who partakes in ceremony knows. When he returns, he is an old man with these teachings in the form of ways to live, values—humility, *dbaadendiziwin*; bravery, *askwa'ode'ewin*; honesty, *gwekwaadziwin*; wisdom, *kbwaakaawin*; truth, *debwewin*; respect, *mnaadendimowin*; and love, *zaagidwin*. Each of these ways are represented by one of our animal relatives.

He gave the people knowledge of fasting and the vision quest. Eventually, a young boy comes to him, and the old man began teaching him these ways. The boy became very ill. The old man told the women of the village, as the givers of life, to build a lodge of maple saplings. We still use saplings from the maple, *ininitig*, man tree, because it is also a giver of life in the form of sustenance, maple sap.

So, they built a lodge facing the eastern doorway, and there was a door facing the west. The top was kept open, and they placed fern, spruce, and balsam around its sides to represent the nourishment provided by our plant relatives. Water was placed at the eastern doorway. Anyway, it's a long story, but eventually the old man remembered that when he was in the sky, the grandfathers held the teachings in a water drum. All the teachings on how to live were there in the drum. The old man made the water drum from what he remembered he saw when he was in the sky. Today, our ceremonial lodge is built the same way the old man taught the people. The water drum still represents the teachings.

The story is much more in depth than what I can describe, and each detail is very important knowledge for those who are part of our ceremonies. Eventually, however, the old man was given knowledge of how to conduct the first ceremony. All of this took four days. Today the ceremony takes four days to prepare for ceremony.

Uncle did this, conducted the ceremonies, until he was an old, old man. All along the way he had helpers, and one of his helpers carried on when he was too old to lead.

I still go to ceremonies to this day. You'll find me there in the lodge with the elder women. Sometimes I'll do my healings there at ceremonies. Sometimes people will come to my home and offer me tobacco and I will administer the medicines to them.

The people at the hospital where I am volunteering don't know a thing about that part of me, a healer. I suppose they just think I'm an elderly Native woman shuffling down the hallways of the ward, going from room to room, visiting the elderly and reading to children. And I think that sometimes both the young and adults, especially non-Natives, think the elderly like me are just old. So, they tend to ignore us, send us off to senior living. We know things though. I know things, teachings so vast and powerful, and beautiful and everlasting they could not even begin to comprehend.

If they would only be more observant, and learn to listen.

Nowadays though, I see so much suffering among our people I could keep busy twenty-four seven and never be able to serve all of those in need. I say at community gatherings when I'm given the opportunity to do so, the teachings are all inside you. This knowledge I possess, you were born with it as well. You just need to go deep inside yourself and bring it out.

I've been powwowing since day one. My father was lead singer on a drum. My mother was a jingle dress dancer. So, there I was, way back as a little one just beginning to walk, being led by my mother out into the circle of the dance area, teetering, trying to move my feet to the rhythm of the drum. There. My fat little cheeks, chubby hands, golden brown skin, black hair lovingly put in braids by my mother or an auntie, a blue satin dance outfit with yellow and red and black and white ribbons. A pair of moosehide moccasins with floral beadwork. The men around the drum singing just high. And occasionally, one of the men's traditional dancers moving in close to the drummers and sounding his eagle bone whistle, a cue for them to continue their singing because the song was so beautiful, he did not want it to end. All the other dancers soon joining him, men and women waving their eagle feather fans high in the air, caught up in the beautiful, beautiful, mesmerizing songs of our people. Dancing, dancing, from the first warmups on summer Friday evenings until the last song, a traveling song, sung on Sunday afternoons. Then we would carefully pack our outfits into tattered, old suitcases to await another weekend on the powwow trail. Pull the stakes on our tents, take them down and put them back into tent bags. Put all our cooking gear away, fold blankets, stack our pillows on top of them into the back of the old, brown station wagon we called our war pony. Then off we'd go down the dusty, dirt roads of some reservation, way out in the bush somewhere, off to home. And always, it would be dark long before we got there and my father would have to carry us, my sister June and I, fast asleep, into the house and put us to bed.

And we would awaken in the morning and eventually, sleepily, enter the kitchen where our mother and father would be sitting at the table drinking black coffee, talking soft and low in the language. Talking about what a wonderful time they had at powwow. Talking about all the friends and relatives they spent time with while visiting there. And we would walk to them, and climb onto their laps, and they would hug us just tight.

And we would ask, where are we going to powwow next weekend? And our mother and father, one or both of them, would begin a new story of the next powwow. Because everything, the whole circle of our lives was there, and is represented in the circle of the dance area at powwows. And all of it is story.

Because that is what life is, story. You are story, I am story. Each of us, all together.

When I was older and had my own family, and my own blue (my favorite color) station wagon, I continued on the powwow trail. Red Lake Fourth of July Powwow, *Miigwich* Mahnomen Days in Ball Club, the traditional powwow in Inger, Sobriety Powwow in Sawyer on the Fond du Lac Rez, Veterans powwow there at Fond du Lac again, Rendezvous Days way up in Grand Portage, Hinckley Powwow, Bad River Traditional Powwow. Every weekend of summer putting miles on that old war pony. Living on hot dogs and Cheeto's and camp coffee and fry bread cooked in lard over the campfire.

There with my husband and little girls. Two of them just like my sister June and I. My girls, dancers as well, in outfits I hand-stitched for them. My husband, at first a young fancy dancer, and when he got older and his knees started to go, a men's traditional dancer. He always took first or second place in his category. We'd met at the Red Lake powwow. I told him I fell for him because he was the best dancer out there, besides me. He teased almost as good as me, I told him.

His name was Bill. He was a good man and we were in love. I'll tell you more about him later.

We made things to trade, sell at the powwows, to help cover our expenses and give us some extra spending cash. I sewed women's dance outfits, shawls for the girls and women made of satin with the extra-long fringe, ribbon shirts for the men, leggings, beaded earrings, bracelets, hair ties, ankle bracelets. My husband worked deer and moosehide, moccasins mostly, upon which he beaded our Ojibwe woodland designs in all the beautiful colors.

We never set up as vendors at the powwows. We just had this reputation for making good products, and word got around, so people would come to our tent when we were there and we'd have our wares spread out on the ground on a Pendleton blanket with price tags on them. Most of our sales were cash. We made enough for gas money, food, and for keeping our old war pony humming down the road, and sometimes we'd trade for wares when one of the customers didn't have the money to pay for something. I especially liked trading for food commodities, those cans of government peanut butter and spam, powdered eggs, commodity cheese, and those cans of meat we called Gravy Train, that I always thought were horse meat but tasted so darn good. Flour and lard for making fry bread. Usually after every powwow we'd be roaring down the road toward home with a box of commods, as we called them, government food.

I've had a good life. There isn't much I can complain about. I've suffered, of course, like all of us do. Life is that way. Not a one of us walks through life unscathed. We all carry our own burdens, our own demons, challenges, some of us a lot more than others. I don't usually bring up my own. Sometimes, though, they come back to visit me, you know, in dreams. My husband would have to awaken me in the middle of the night when this happened.

"Babe," he'd say, nudging me softly. "Wake up, Babe."

He loved me. He did. And I loved him.

Still, sometimes out on the powwow trail I'd find myself searching the faces of the other dancers, singers, those in the crowd. And then I would return, in memory, to late evenings, to the songs of the peepers, to a field of wildflowers and sage and red clover behind the sister school.

Sometimes that longing to see him, hear his voice.

And sometimes only in dreams.

Simon.

CHAPTER THREE
St. Mary's Mission School

Simon

I was one of the youngest of the children in my family. My sister Annie and brother Johnny were closest to me in age. Some of the older ones were already gone and living adult lives when I was still in primary school. Most all were sent off to the government run or sponsored boarding and mission schools, except in summers, and sometimes during Christmas break when we would all walk into town, my father, mother, and meet them at the Tulip Shop, a café that also served as the bus station. I remember my older sisters and brothers who were still of school age, Johnny, Annie, Faith, Patty, Joshua, and Beau coming in on the bus a day or two apart, carrying their government issued overnight bags holding all their worldly possessions. My older sisters and brothers, Alexis, Terry, George, Mike, Robert, and Jim, all out of school and off into the world somewhere. Some working jobs, some looking for work, one spending his life drinking out in the bush on the side of the hill overlooking town with his friends.

When summers or Christmas breaks were over, we'd all walk back into town and send the ones still in school off again, my mother crying. My father, there on the sidewalk, stoic, arms down at his sides, body shifting from side to side, looking down at the ground.

Sometimes I wish I had asked my father and mother why they were all sent away to those schools in the first place. That maybe they could have all gone to the local public schools in town. I know there they would have had to put up with town kids calling them every possible racial slur in the book—timber niggers, wagon burners, Injuns, squaws. There, where the teachers wouldn't have expected much of them because they just saw them as bush Indians. Maybe my siblings would have been able to ignore the taunts, maybe they would have fought back, issued a few bloody noses so the white kids were afraid of them. Maybe if schooling would have been easy for them, they could have been one of the smartest kids in their class and they could have been the teacher's pet, and the white kids would have called them "honest" Injuns, not like the other bush Indians who had to put up with the daily, racist torment out in the playground, or in the hallways. Who were expected to not amount to much by the teachers, to drop out as soon as they reached legal age, or to get pregnant from some town boy who said they were beautiful, who would abandon them when their belly began to swell.

Maybe my parents figured they wouldn't have been welcomed there in the public school. Maybe they suffered the same indignities when they went to town, in the stores and other businesses. Or, maybe there were simply too many mouths to feed at home. After all, our father barely made enough cutting wood to make ends meet. The times we lived in were long before government issued food commodities, food stamps, feeding centers, food shelves. We had to make due with what we could get out of the river, bush, gardens. And, maybe, that wasn't enough.

Or maybe our parents believed the lies told to us by the Indian agent, who told them only good things would come from sending their children off to those schools. That they would be well prepared to enter the adult world, to read, write, and cipher. To speak educated English, and therefore be accepted into society. To get away from the reservation, live in Chicago, Cleveland, Minneapolis. Make a good wage, buy a house and a decent car. Forget about reservation life.

I swore to myself that life would be different for me. I'd go to the public school, put up with whatever I had to. My whole world was there on Reservation Road, the trails leading to the river, the hills. My father, mother, aunties and uncles were all there in that place. I felt protected there, loved.

So, when I was six years old and it was time for me to start my schooling, and the Indian agent was to come to the house during the summer before the start of school, I ran and hid in the bush, down one of the trails that led to the river, where I spent the day throwing rocks in the water until I was bored silly, then took a nap under a tree until late afternoon and was getting too hungry to stay any longer and walked back up the hill to home.

And I tried to sneak in the house just quiet, but my mother caught me, a board in the kitchen floor giving me away with a creak.

"Son," she said. "The Indian agent was here today to talk school. He said you have your choice. You can go to Flandreau, Pipestone or St. Mary's Mission. They're all down in Dakota country, but that's where most of our kind go for their schooling, so you won't be alone there."

All of this in our language. Now as an old man I think of our beautiful language and how, at that moment my mother spoke to me all those years ago, it hurt. Each word cut deep into my heart.

"I won't go," I said. "I'll run away."

I'd hardly ever been off the reservation. My only trips to town had been to meet or send off my older sisters and brothers to those schools.

"I'll move in with Auntie and Uncle," I said. "They'll never find me that way."

I had an Auntie and Uncle who lived far out in the bush, rarely came into town. Lived off fish from the river, deer meat, wild rice. Spoke no English.

"Oh, son," she said. "What are we going to do with you?"

She gestured for me to come to her, I remember. And held me as I cried.

"I don't want to go, *ni mamaa*, mother."

I, the stubborn one. Every family, it seems, has one.

"I don't want to go."

That night after my father came home from work, we had a sit down, my mother, father, and I. My siblings, Annie and Johnny, sent into the bedroom and told to stay there until they were told they could come out. They would stay there, playing. Back then, when Ojibwe children knew, by that look, or the pursing and sideways movement, pointing of the lips, they were to disappear until they were told it was time to reappear. Back when their only toys were hand-me-down dolls and battered push cars or trucks. Back before VR headsets and hand-held video games. Back before young people even dared talk back and disobey a parent. Back when fathers rarely had to, only if need be, took a stick of kindling wood to the rear of an unusually insolent child.

There at the kitchen table, the room lit by a gas lamp, my father rolling a cigarette, then lighting it from the hot chimney of the lamp. My mother, there, still wearing her apron from cooking dinner, doing dishes.

"So, your mother tells me you want to go to the public school there in town," he said.

"I do," I said quietly, eyes facing downward,

"And why is that?" he asked. "All your older brothers and sisters went or are going to the government schools. The agent came to the house when it was their time. They went. They didn't say they wanted to go to the public school."

"The kids from here who go to the town school," he said. "Have troubles there."

"But I want to," I said. "I want to try it, anyways."

I always spoke respectfully to my father and mother. I never, ever raised my voice to either of them once during their lifetimes. That was the way we were back then, back when our ways were still strong. My eyes facing downward, looking just hard at the floor.

Then silence for what seemed like the longest time, me knowing there was great meaning in silence, when there were no words that needed to be spoken.

"Then you can give it a try," he said.

And I did.

***

So, I started school in the fall. Rode the reservation bus to the public school. The oldest, most decrepit bus in the fleet, only good enough for the Native children, driven by a driver who didn't care for Native people. Me and twenty some other stubborn children who refused to be sent off to the government or mission schools, who were willing to face being ostracized because of the color of our skin and reservation English, teased for smelling like wood-smoke or number two fuel oil or fry bread grease. There, sitting on the bus and in the back of classrooms dressed in hand-me-down clothes, shoes from the boxes of freebies at the back of the church. There, too poor to afford school lunches. There, with homemade bread smeared with lard or bacon grease sandwiches, wrapped in wax paper in crumbled paper bags. There, with no pencils or paper or erasers, or store-bought note books. There, with black hair and dark brown eyes among a sea of blonde, blue-eyed children of German or Scandinavian immigrants. There, strangers, unwanted in the land of their ancestors. There, teachers who spoke loudly and slowly and over enunciated every word spoken to them like we couldn't understand their words, like we were deaf or somehow challenged, or both. Who did the same thing to our parents if they came at all to parent-teacher conferences, and wondered why they never came again.

So, I had to put up with some of that in school. However, schoolwork and I became good friends. The written word flowed from me like fresh, bubbling spring water. Math was easy. I memorized all the states and their capitals, knew all and more of what I needed to know about George Washington, Abraham Lincoln, and the founding fathers. I even tried to join orchestra, play the violin, but sister Annie and brother Johnny teased me out of it when I took the instrument home to practice. Teachers were surprised by me, the smart one.

And I became an "honest" Injun to the town boys.

"You're not like the rest of them Injuns," they would say to me. "You're an honest Injun."

I, the honest Injun. Proud, head held just high. Fool.

I did this well into the sixth grade. Twelve years old, the smart one riding the reservation bus to school and back each day, playing alone out in the playground.

———◆———

The playground at my school was a big, scary place. And it seemed that at every recess, a group of town boys would tease a younger Native boy who rode the reservation bus with the rest of us "Injuns," as they called us, into school each day. Their words were sharp as knives, incessant. "Hey, squaw boy! You gonnum scalp us?" He would plead with them to stop, but they would continue their taunting until he cried uncontrollably and chased them all over the playground. Ultimately, he would tire and then cower in a corner like a wounded fawn, and his tormenters would encircle him like jackals and kill his spirit with the sharp spears of their tongues. Only once do I remember he caught one of them and beat holy bejesus out of him. When I saw this, the inside me, the part that never showed, rose and gave him a standing ovation.

Most of the time, however, he would suffer the poison of their words. I remember as I watched and listened to the daily, awful scene, my stomach muscles would tighten and sometimes I would almost bend over in pain. I wanted to say something to them, to yell at them, beg of them. "Leave him alone. Please leave him alone, he has done nothing to you."

But I never said a word. I was stopped cold by fear. Fear that they would turn on me, that I would become their target.

So, the years passed, and the unrelenting torment continued. And then one day, when I was in the sixth grade, he just quit coming to school. Myself, I had grown in stature and confidence, and became good with my fists.

I was not teased.

I remember years later reading the hometown newspaper and noticed his name in the obituary column. He died young. I don't know the circumstances. His former tormenters had become the city fathers—city councilmen, business owners, bankers, and teachers. Hopefully they learned from the folly of their past.

And me, living homeless on the streets in Minneapolis, or in a rooming house, somewhere between drunken stupors and sobriety, shelters, one room tenement apartments, day labor.

Me, the smart one.

In the summer when I turned thirteen, having just completed the sixth grade, I made the decision to change schools. I'd had enough, I suppose, and saw nothing ahead of me but the same old thing. When the Indian agent showed his face at our door, I was there waiting for him.

I remember talking with my father about my change of heart. He, who was forcibly taken from his parents at the age of six and sent to a mission school somewhere in Wisconsin, and didn't see his mother or father again until he was twelve years old, spending his summers working on farms. His parents, my grandparents, illiterate, lived the old ways. No letters, no transport to the school for visits. No word for many years. He, beaten for speaking the language, made to kneel on hard peas for hours as punishment. He, watching children around him die of loneliness, buried out back behind the school. Children running away, freezing to death. Letters send back to the Indian agent of their home communities to have him inform parents that their children were gone. Then at twelve years old, he ran away. Slept in ditches, stole food from gardens, walked, ran, caught rides.

"I never went back," he said.

How could he now tell us, his own children, that we should go to those schools after what he had to endure?

Now when the Indian agent came to the house, he wore a smile. Offered a firm handshake. Told my father and mother that the schools were not the same as when they were young. That things are better now. The teachers are good. They like Native children. The food is good. There's a lot of it. They'll get to go to town on Saturdays with their friends. They'll get to come home during Christmas break and summers. And on and on, and my father believed him. The agent, smiling.

"Here you go, sign this form, right here," he said. "We'll bring over a bus ticket for him the end of August."

Those two faces our ancestors spoke about in our prophecies. That the light-skinned race would come and we wouldn't know if he was wearing the face of brotherhood or the face of death because both would look the same.

We were fools.

That smile was not a smile.

"Where do you want to go?" He asked. "There are openings at Flandreau and St. Mary's Mission down by Granite Falls. You can go to either one, your choice."

I had heard stories about Flandreau from some of the kids that returned from there. How sometimes the Dakota and Ojibwe didn't get along, girls and boys. Dirty looks became fist fights, hair pulling.

Me, a good Catholic boy. An altar boy at the church up Reservation Road.

"St. Mary's Mission," I said.

The stories of our lives are written along the way in a journey made of both conscious and unconscious decisions. We travel a path. It comes to a divide. We ask ourselves if we should go this way or that. And, sometimes we just unconsciously take a left or right, or keep moving straightaway. A few of us have a destination in mind, but many of us take the meandering way, simply allowing life to happen.

Now an old man, I wonder what would have become of me if I had chosen to stay at home and continue my education at the public school. What would have become of me? Maybe I would have eventually exploded from the obvious racism there, from being invisible to the teachers. Or perhaps, being a school boy, I may have eventually been allowed some acceptance by the mainstream. To be the Indian friend. To be the pet Indian of a teacher. To be chosen for one of the year-end academic awards. To graduate near the top of my class in front of a surprised audience of parents, grandparents and, other relatives of town kids gathered in the school gymnasium for commencement. Who is that Indian boy there, they would ask? There with the brown skin, black hair? There among a sea of blonde, blue-eyed, smiling faces, with sparkling, white teeth. Who is that?

Or maybe I would have caved, imploded, grown weary. Maybe I would have decided to leave school when I became of legal age to do so. Gotten a job at one of the mills in town, became a logger like my father. Married one of the local reservation girls, had a dozen kids, become fat on deer meat soup with potatoes.

I chose. In the end, the path led me over two hundred miles southwest of home, deep in prairie country. Me, the smart, good Catholic boy.

I remember to this day when my mother and father, sister Annie and brother Johnny walked me down to the bus depot in town. My mother had packed me a meal for the journey, homemade bread and strawberry jam we had gathered and canned earlier in the summer. Two boiled eggs. A slice of cake, no frosting. A jug of tea.

We walked down Reservation Road, then took a path through the bush, down the hill to the railroad tracks that ran alongside the river, then into town. Me, carrying a tattered old carryon used by one of my older brothers when he went off to school. Filled with two changes of clothes, cleaned and freshly ironed, as new as one could find in the boxes of free clothes in the room in the back of the church. Donated by families of well-meaning townspeople, good Christian folk. Walking with my family, past the large, white homes in town, the ones with green and blue and black shutters of the town's mill executives, past the furniture stores and gas stations, the fire hall and police station, a movie theatre I had never been to, because we could never have afforded it. And when we drew near the depot my mother took my hand and we walked the rest of the way. She reached in her purse and withdrew two crumpled dollar bills.

"You might need this," she said.

I don't remember ever having so much money in my life.

My father. A quiet man. Words didn't come easy for him.

"My boy," he said. "You take care of yourself there at that school. Show them what you're made of."

We stood waiting on the sidewalk for the bus, a hot August sun bearing down upon us. And eventually we saw the bus pull around the corner, come to a stop in front of us, its air brakes hissing, smelling of diesel, the low rumble of its motor. The door swung open and two passengers disembarked, the driver opening the luggage door and handing them their suitcases.

"You coming, boy?" He turned to me. I handed him my bag.

My mother hugging me. Her face buried in my chest, shirt wet from her tears. My father, standing there, stoic, hands at his sides. Sister Annie and brother Johnny standing there as well, fidgeting, squinting from the sun.

And, me. The smart one.

⁕⁕⁕

I sat in front, not wanting to miss a thing. We stopped in other small towns along the way. People getting on, getting off. Moose Lake, Willow River, Sandstone. In Hinckley three other Native kids got on the bus. They climbed aboard and saw me, one of their kind going off to school. Then off one highway and onto another toward St. Cloud. Stops in Mora and Foley. In St. Cloud we had a transfer. There, another group of Native kids, probably having come down from Red Lake, White Earth, Leech Lake Reservations. Not a one of us speaking to each other, avoiding eye contact. I, afraid of missing the bus to Granite Falls. The other Native boys and girls and I, sitting on the benches of the bus depot in downtown St. Cloud. Sitting there waiting to go to school, to be educated by teachers who liked Native kids, to nuns and a priest that told us we were all children of God, all of us, no matter our skin, or whether we were rich or poor. God loves you, Native child, they would say.

Soon enough the bus enters the station. People climb aboard. We wait, all of us young Native passengers, until everyone else is on the bus. Respectful that way. We were taught well at home.

I get a window seat, watch the land open up. Fields of corn for miles, as far as I could see. Nibbling on my sandwich, drinking my tea. Saving my cake for last.

Then hours later, dusk, the sun low in the sky, and I barely hanging on, that world somewhere between awake and asleep. The sound of the air brakes, lurching to a stop.

By now, some twenty of us Native students waiting to disembark, waiting for the others, being respectful the way we were taught.

Then it's my turn. I rise and walk down the narrow row of the bus, step down the stairs and out onto a dirt parking lot.

There, in the corner of my eye an old yellow school bus out across the street, emblazoned on its side, "St. Mary's Mission School." A tall Native man, dressed in black, standing next to it.

And greeting us as we disembark the bus, one of the school matrons. Native, a Dakota woman I presume. Motioning with her lips for us to proceed across the street to the yellow bus. Speaking in that familiar sing song, low and sweet, broken English.

We all climb aboard. Quiet, no one speaking, all looking out across the fields, rumbling down a narrow dirt road. Then ahead, among a gathering of cottonwood trees, a church and other buildings, all of wood and yellow sandstone.

Now just getting dark, we have arrived.

A priest standing there as we disembark, arms folded across his chest, smiling slightly.

"I'm Father Adrian," he says to us in perfect English.

"Welcome to St. Mary's."

CHAPTER FOUR

Bakaanige

Carolina

Now as an old woman, I'm considered an elder in the Native community. That means I go to the clinic a lot. My doctor at the reservation's urban clinic in Duluth has prescribed a whole medicine chest of pills for me to take to keep me breathing, ticking, walking Duluth's steep hills, shuffling up and down the stairs of my apartment without losing my breath and keeling over dead. All are just supplements, because apparently, old people need them for some reason. Iron because of a deficiency, Calcium for my bones, Vitamin C to help my body absorb the iron, Vitamin D3 for winter blues, fish pills, a multivitamin, Ocuvite for macular degeneration. She has me going to the clinic every other month, it seems, to pound on my back, hold a freezing stethoscope to my chest and back, have me pee in a little container, draw blood. Then, after I'm done, I get to sit in the pharmacy waiting area for a big bag of prescriptions. After I get them, I walk up the steep hills of Duluth a couple of blocks with that bag of pills shaking like a rattle. Those hills keep me in shape.

I don't want to make her feel bad but I don't take any of the pills she prescribes to me. I know she is a healer like me, and I respect that. However, I'm also a healer. I gather and prescribe our natural medicines. Those are the medicines I take, the ones gathered from the bush. Every day I have one of them big soup cups of tea I brew from a mushroom that grows on birch trees. Put a little maple syrup in it to sweeten it up a bit. We use that for just about anything, headaches, fevers, diabetes, heart disease. Our ancestors have been using the natural medicines forever. They learned all the medicines by asking the spirits, in dreams, and by watching our animal relatives. Animals have gathered and used medicines for thousands and thousands of years.

Sometimes when I'm sitting in the clinic lobby waiting to see my doctor I'll run into another elder waiting, like me, who is there to be poked and prodded, and scolded because we eat too many sweets. And if they can talk in the language we'll be going back and forth. The ladies who work reception must not speak *Ojibwemowin* because one of them asked me one time if we were talking about them, and I said, *eya'*, yes, and smiled at her and laughed. I don't know if she believed me or not. Even our own Native people, some of them anyway, don't understand our humor. Anyway, we weren't. We talk the language because we can. It just feels good to speak it. Sometimes it's a reminder for me of the days when we all spoke it.

Anyway, the medicines I prescribe to myself and walking the hills of Duluth keep me pretty healthy. I think I'll live for a while longer.

My reservation, Leech Lake, is pretty good to me as well. At Christmastime we elders get a ham, Thanksgiving a turkey. Sometimes we'll get the fixings as well, a box of instant potatoes, cans of sweet potatoes and cranberries, Stovetop stuffing. They have a senior advocate bring a vanload of it down from Cass Lake and deliver it to the Indian center on Second Street and all we have to do is go there and pick it up. And once we load up, the center loans us some young person to help us lug it all home if we don't have a vehicle, or a ride. I live just up the street a couple of blocks so it's no problem. It's quite a deal.

I really appreciate how our Native community, many of them anyway, treats us elders, takes care of us. Put us up in front of the line when there are feasts, bring us food plates at powwows, give up their seats for us, if need be, offer us *asemaa*, tobacco, when they want our advice about something, or need our language skills to say the offering at an event.

Imagine that. It seems just yesterday I was a little girl running down the trail to the lake through the bush with my sister June, jumping into the water, splashing each other, laughing. Sitting next to my father on the couch at night when he would talk story about when he was young, or if it was winter, when he'd tell the winter stories, the ones we can only tell when there is snow on the ground. Or when he would carry me to my bed when I fell asleep listening my parents talk, or when I was listening to the radio. My mother holding me on her lap when I was sick with a cold or fever.

Life goes so quickly, it seems.

I learned a lot from my parents, aunties, and uncles, when I was young. When a neighbor, or an auntie or uncle would come over at night to visit and my parents would gather with them in the kitchen over coffee, they would send June and I into our bedroom to play. June had her dolls, and she could spend hours with them, talking to them and for them, having pretend tea parties. She never seemed interested in what was going on in the next room. Not me, I'd be lying on the floor next to a wide-open door, listening. I'm a listener, you see. I've learned a lot that way. The adults, just several feet away, talking story, all in the language. Laughing and teasing each other, as well.

Just think how different the world would be if there was more listening.

Anyway, they'd all know I was there lying on the floor listening to their every word, of course. And when my aunties or uncles would get up to leave, sometimes after hours of drinking coffee and talking story, they would call for me before they left for their homes. June would be long gone by then, sleeping curled up on the bed with her dolls.

"Come here, my girl." That's what they called me. One of my aunties would open her arms to give me a hug, an uncle would rub my back.

I never, ever disrespected my elders. When they approached me, I never looked them straightaway in the eyes. That was considered disrespectful. Always, my eyes down, I would speak to them in a soft voice. When they would take their leave, I would tell them goodbye. My mother said when we do that, we are telling them they are welcome to return.

"Goodbye, Auntie. Goodbye Uncle." I would go to a window and watch as they departed, and wave to them.

Kindness was always stressed. My mother would have me bring jam to an elderly neighbor, or a widower. If she knew someone was ill, she would make soup and have me deliver it, knock on their door, until I heard someone coming to open it, and leave it on the steps, standing back so as to not get ill myself. I liked my mother's soup as well, *waboose naboob*, rabbit soup, and *baka-aquay minawaa mahnomen naboob*, chicken and wild rice soup. Her and the others back then ate rabbit head soup, I remember. Me, I could never get into it. When my mother was older and she knew I was cleaning rabbit to make soup, she would say,

"Save the heads."

I'd do it, but only for her. Rabbit heads and I just don't see eye to eye, no pun intended.

My mother rarely ever raised her voice.

"Kindness," she said. "That's number one. That is above all the most important thing in treating others. When you do that, it will return back to you throughout your whole lifetime."

It's not that I was the perfect child. Every once in a while, I got that look, the one my mother learned from her mother, when she needed to let me know to behave, quit fighting my sister. And only once I remember my father going to the woodpile to fetch a stick of kindling, when both June and I got a swat on our behinds because June talked me into throwing crabapples at passing cars.

When my girls were bad, I gave them that look as well. And my husband Bill, he had to make more than one trip out the kindling pile with them, one more than the other. The stubborn one. We all seem to have one.

———————

I can remember back a long way. My first memory I'm in my Indian swing, that's what my parents called it anyway, made from a blanket folded over into a cradle and pinned between two ropes that were hung above my parent's bed. The blanket was held apart with two sticks of kindling wood, one on each end, and I was in it, swinging back and forth as one of my parents gave it a gentle push every once in a while. I remember it was summer and the window was open and there was a breeze coming in and there were sheer curtains that were moving back and forth. I couldn't have been more than two years old.

In daytime, my mother kept me in a *dikinogan*, cradle board, made by one of my uncles, when I was little. She said just after I was born, she put my navel cord into a deerskin pouch that hung over me in the *dikinogan*, to show the life connection between her, as mother, and me, as her child. After a year, she said, she took the pouch out into the bush and buried it, to show that from then on, I would become my own individual, and one day move on to become an adult, have my own babies.

In the *dikinogan*, she said, I could travel with her when she was doing her outside work, in the garden, or washing clothes on a scrub board or with an old, gas-powered wringer washer. There I would be with her, she said, propped up against a tree, or the side of the house. Sometimes, she said, she would give me a small lump of maple sugar cake to suck on, wrapped in cloth, if I was fussy or teething.

When I was older, I asked my mother if I could have the *dikinogan* for my own girls, and she gave it to me. I used it with them as well. I put their navel cords in deer hide pouches that hung over them. When they were a year old, I brought it out into the bush. I gave my baby girls "sugar tit," that's what we called it in English, maple sugar cakes, wrapped in cloth, when they were fussy or teething.

There, out in my garden, or out in the berry patches in the bush, my girls also learned by watching me, and observing all of life around them. My mother said that is how we teach young ones to listen, observe. She said it helps them dream, that dreams are a baby's first visions. And when my girls became mothers as well, I passed the *dikinogan* down to them. I made the deer skin pouches for my grandbabies, the ones that held their navel cords. Our ways continue that way.

As I grew into a little girl, I began helping her with women's work. Gardening, washing clothes and hanging them on the line, cooking, cleaning the house. This came early, when I was six, seven years old. She taught me to sew, darn, knit. I boiled cleaning jars and helped her pick the crop and can, make jams and jellies from the berries we harvested from the bush. I learned that work was something all of us must do. That it was part of being a family. My sister June learned work as well, although often begrudgingly, as she always seemed to be wearing a pout whenever she was asked to do her part, to learn how to do a task. Invariably, she would complain, never in front of our mother of course, but to me, when we were alone.

She's always been like that, ever since she was a child. Sometimes I think she came out of the womb that way, complaining about conditions inside our mother. Even now as an old woman she sometimes has more negative things to say about things, or people, than good.

I try not to listen to her when she gets that way, though. I put on my inner ear muffs.

"Blah, blah, blah." That's all I hear whenever she starts to get on my nerves.

I had my first menses when I was twelve years old. My mother and one of my aunties helped through the *bakaanige*, the isolation that is held for girls when they have their first period. During our menses, we are spiritually very powerful, they said, and must be separated from others.

Mother and Auntie built a small wigwam for me out in the bush behind the house that was big enough for me to lie down in. There I was for eight days. Before I went into the wigwam, they blackened my cheeks and forehead with warm charcoal and tied my hair back. My mother combed my hair. Each day, my mother would come and hand feed me. I was not allowed to touch food or feed myself during my isolation. Even a year after the *bakaanige*, I washed and dried my own utensils during my cycle.

This is what my Auntie said about the power I had during my menses: "You should not touch plants. Your power is very great. The plants will wither and die. Do not go near the lake, streams, or rivers. The fish will become ill and die. Do not look directly at another person. Do not cross the path of another person. You are so powerful you could harm them. Do not touch the clothes of your father, or your uncles. Don't touch regalia or sacred items, or be near the drum."

Mother and Auntie taught me many, many things about living while I was in that wigwam. They told me about my responsibilities of being a woman, about living in a good way.

When I was allowed out of the wigwam, my mother and auntie led me back home. They had laid cedar boughs on the path for me to walk upon, to protect others who might cross the path. There, my father had prepared a feast of things he had gathered. Deer meat, fish, fry bread, and things that were ripe for the season.

And at the feast where my aunties and uncles and parents were all gathered, my mother announced that I, Carolina Shaugobay, *Anung*, Star, was now to be considered a woman, because I, like other women, was now able to be a creator of life itself.

When my girls had their first menses, I too built them a small wigwam out in the bush and did all the things my mother and auntie taught me. And when their girls had their first menses, they did the same. The circle continues that way.

I hear nowadays that some mothers check their girls into the Holiday Inn or casino hotel to do their *bakaanige*.

Holaay, I'm thinking. That's rez English for "what next."

⟶⟶

Both my sister June and I went through grade school at the Greenwood School, a two-room wooden schoolhouse several miles up the Old Cass Lake Highway toward Bemidji. Most of our fellow students were reservation kids, but we had a few white kids as well. We got along, most of us anyway. In thinking back I'd guess the white kids felt outnumbered so they didn't dare say anything bad about us Natives. We didn't have to walk two miles uphill each way through the snow like some elders teasingly say about how tough they had it back then. We rode a rickety old school bus that would squeak to a stop right in front of our driveway. I'd always try to find a window seat so I could be looking out. June had her friends, and they were always in the back laughing, talking, and making too much noise. There were many times the driver, a balding white man with a gruff voice and a face that forgot how to smile had to look back in the rear-view mirror and tell them to quiet it down.

"You girls shut up back there," he'd yell. And June would always reply in a voice just above a whisper, so he wouldn't be able to hear.

"You shut up, up there." And the girls would all laugh.

June never got the respect thing down well, I guess. She was always kind of a smart aleck.

I can't say I learned a lot in elementary school. My classroom had kindergarten through sixth grade. Mrs. Bushy was the teacher. She was a middle-aged white lady. Most of her time was spent trying to teach the younger ones how to read, write, and cipher. As we moved up in grades, we became her helpers, reading to the younger ones or helping them with addition and subtraction.

I just know that come sixth grade I'd have to make a decision one way or the other about where I would be going for grade seven. The closest high school was in Bemidji, some fifteen miles away. Bemidji was a big town, the main city in all of northwestern Minnesota, and the high school had nearly three hundred students in each grade level. I was dreading the idea of it all. I was much more comfortable among a small group and the thought of being surrounded by swarms of students, and being only a few Native students among a sea of non-Natives didn't sound appealing in the least.

At the end of sixth grade, the Indian agent showed up at our place and talked with my parents about sending me off to one of the boarding and mission schools. Among many of the platitudes he would say about the schools was the fact some were small, with only several hundred students.

"Flandreau and Pipestone are the larger of the schools," he said, "with over five hundred students apiece. St. Mary's Mission is smaller."

My parents were skeptical of sending us off to the schools because they were both products of the boarding schools. My mother and father had met at Flandreau Indian School back in the days when Native children were beaten for speaking the language or practicing their ways. Neither was allowed to return home at the end of their years there. My father was sent to work on farms during summers. My mother was as well, although during several summers she stayed at the school and worked the garden there, and did housekeeping. They were taken at the age of six and neither saw home until they were sixteen years old.

"I couldn't wait until I was legal age to leave there," my mother had said. Both returned back home to family they hadn't seen in ten years.

"I just remember my mother just held me and cried for the longest time, rocking me back and forth. I was a young lady when I returned. Neither of my parents spoke a word of English, and my Ojibwe tongue had gotten pretty rusty, and it took a while before we could really communicate well. We had spoken our language at the school in secret, late at night and whenever we felt safely away from the teachers, head of the school, or matrons."

She continued.

"We had been told our language and way of worshipping our Creator was the devil's work," she said. "That we were pagans. They made us go to their church every Sunday and learn their ways."

"I remember when I finally returned home," my mother said, "how it felt in my heart to be around our language and ways again, to be among my parents, uncles, and aunties. One of the first things my parents did was take me into ceremony. I cried when she brought me into the teaching lodge and reintroduced me to all our relatives who were there."

My father didn't speak of his time in boarding school. When I was older, I asked him to tell me about it, and he patted me on my head, like he would do when I was a little girl. And he shook his head, no.

"My girl," he would say. "Not now."

My father would go to his grave without sharing his boarding school story with me.

So, the Indian agent had to do a good sell job with my parents before they would even consider sending one of their own children to the boarding school.

I didn't need much convincing. My choice was to go to Granite Falls, St. Mary's Mission School.

Two years later when it came time for my sister June to consider where she would attend high school, she chose the public school in Bemidji because that is where her friends were planning on attending. June and I have always been different. She preferred speaking English among her friends and would often complain to me about being bored at ceremonies and summer powwows. Me, I've always been Ojibwe through and through.

I pleaded with my parents to allow me to go to St. Mary's. And I must have eventually worn them down, because in the end they reluctantly agreed that come fall, that is where I would go.

———————

The summer I was to leave it seemed I was glued to my mother's side, knowing I would only see her at Christmas time and summers. And she must have realized it as well, because she took me with her everywhere. Out in the bush to gather her herbs and medicines. Each time we were out there, she would tell me, reiterate, the use for each plant. We would sing the songs required for harvesting, the prayers that were said to the spirits and our Creator. We gathered birchbark and *weegoob*, basswood twine, for making baskets. We'd sell them at the summer powwows. We picked strawberries, blueberries, and chokecherries for making jellies and jams. We worked the garden, planting, weeding, picking, canning. Come August, she took me out onto my parent's favorite ricing lake to tie the stalks of wild rice so it would be easier to harvest. I would miss the harvest, and the finishing of the rice, parching and dancing it, and most of all, eating it.

One of the things I'd miss terribly at mission school was eating wild rice with bacon grease. I still make it today whenever someone gives me some rice. I raised my girls on it, and they did the same with their children.

Wild rice, she said, was a spirit, given to the Ojibwe by our Creator. It was in ceremony, there in the teaching lodge, where I had learned the story of wild rice, the food that grows on water, and its significance for our people, and the story of our migration from the east to seek it. How our ancestors first came upon it in what is today known as the St. Louis River as it entered Lake Superior. How when it was found, one of our prophecies was fulfilled.

My girls learned the whole story of it when I took them to ceremonies. My grandchildren did the same.

"When you become a mother," my mother had said, "You teach my grandchildren these things as well."

"I will," I said. And I did.

I remembered all the things she taught me to this day. When I became a mother, I taught my girls these things. And as a grandmother, when my grandchildren would visit, I would try to bring them out into the bush to teach them. I realize I wasn't as successful with them. They seemed more interested in their toys and television. They never picked up enough of the language to be fluent, just learning the basics—hello, goodbye, counting to ten, learning the words to all the common animals.

All of that seems to be changing now, of course. They are teaching all of those things in the tribal schools nowadays. How to gather wild rice and make maple syrup, spear fish, choke rabbits, bead, learn the language, hear them traditional stories. The winter stories I learned from my elders when I was young are now being put to writing, in books, so they will be preserved and remembered. The times have changed. I'm just not sure it's for the better. Back when I was young, we lived those ways. Nowadays, it seems we've formalized our teachings into a curriculum. In the end, I suppose, that is how we will continue our ways, and I have to make peace with it.

When I'm sitting at a powwow, I just smile sometimes at our young ones, when they come up to me and offer to get me a food plate. They are trying their best to learn the old ways.

"Auntie," they'll say. "Can I get you a meal?"

Auntie. A word when used among our people that shows the greatest respect for an elder female.

I long for the days when I would take my girls out into the bush and show them our ways, when I would teach them in our language without having to offer an English translation, when the people attending ceremonies, all spoke our language fluently. I'm just old fashioned, I guess, out of date.

I went to summer ceremony before I went off to school, and of course, we traveled to every weekend powwow we could. And at every one I danced so much from Friday night warmups through the Sunday afternoon traveling song I near wore a hole in my moccasins. And at each one, I volunteered to bring food plates to elders and helped walk the elder ones who needed assistance make their ways to a place to sit in the stands.

My mother and father taught me well. I tried to do the same with my girls and for the most part, they did the same when they were parents. Their children, my grandchildren, not so much, I guess. They go to the powwows, of course, but seem to spend all their time there walking the circle outside the powwow grounds with their friends, stopping occasionally to get money from their parents, and me, for an ice cream or other treat.

Sometimes I think about how my life might have been different if my parents had decided to keep me home and sent me to the public school in Bemidji, or if I wouldn't have pleaded with them to allow me to go. Or if I had become like my sister June and been reluctantly Ojibwe. Or, if I wouldn't have done this or hadn't done that, but done this or that instead. We go through life this way. We all seem to be like that, us humans.

Now, as an old woman, I often think back to the summer before I went off to St. Mary's Mission, of pleading with my parents about allowing me to go, getting to spend every day, it seemed, with my mother. Her voice, soft and sweet and low. There, bent down among the plants far out in the bush for an herb, or medicine. Offering that *asemaa*, tobacco, to the spirits and our Creator, before she would harvest. There, helping me with my dance outfit at each powwow, combing and putting my hair up with an eagle fluff hair tie. Helping me put on my ankle-length beaded moccasins. There at ceremony, camping out in the bush for four days and nights, there among friends, parents, aunties, uncles, and cousins.

And I remember clearly that warm, August day, when my parents drove me into Bemidji, to the parking lot where the statues of Paul Bunyan and Babe the Blue Ox still stand today on the shoreline of Lake Bemidji. Statues that celebrate the clearcutting of what was once our people's lands, when the area was covered with majestic white pine, when the lakes and rivers were clean and teeming with fish, the bush filled with animals that our people harvested. When this all was Ojibwe country.

I remember when the bus pulled up. Some thirty of us from the nearby reservation communities, Red Lake, Leech Lake, White Earth, waiting along with our parents.

I remember my father, his hand on my back, rubbing it softly, my mother hugging me so tight I had trouble breathing.

"Baby girl," she said, crying softly.

And then, the Indian agent telling us it was time to go. Lined up, one by one, we slowly climbed into the bus and found our seats. I was fortunate enough to find a window seat where I could see my parents and sister June standing there, waving, as we made our way out of the parking lot, making a wide left turn and heading south to the school.

I, thirteen years old, going into the seventh grade.

Singing under my breath.

A traveling song.

CHAPTER FIVE

Amazing Grace

Simon

Even now as an old man, I remember my first days at the sister school.

The first thing after we got off the bus at the school, Father Adrian told us to line up, boys in one row and girls in the other. He read a list of names, and we were told to raise our hands when our name was called.

"Charles Moose, Rodney Black Bear, Cyrus Runs With Him . . ." Each name a young Dakota or Ojibwe boy.

"Patricia Reese, Esther Sam, Mary Ann Two Bulls . . ." Each name a young Dakota or Ojibwe girl.

Each like me. Apprehensive, afraid, alone.

Soon, a nun and matron appeared, marched the girls off to their dormitory.

Father Adrian led the boys to the boys' dorm, where one by one, we were told to sit, a nun and matron awaiting us. Our hair, even the boys who had been there the year or years before was washed with something I'm sure was kerosene.

"We don't want any of you spreading lice," the nun said. The nun, it's been too many years to remember her name. All of the nuns were teachers there. I remember vaguely she was pale as can be with icy blue eyes. She was the one who silently, roughly washed my hair, killed the lice I didn't have. I don't remember much about the matron, except that she was a Native woman, Dakota, I presume because I learned later all the matrons were local women from the Upper Sioux Agency near Granite Falls.

Smelling of kerosene, we were led into the gang showers by Father Adrian.

"Scrub down good," he said. Bar soap, institutional, brown, lye, made there at the school.

The water was cold. I remember it was my first shower. We didn't have running water at home. Our drinking water came from a community pump up the road, and a spring halfway down the hill off the trail leading to the river. Back home, baths were on Sunday evenings. We brothers shared the same water, one by one, in an old galvanized wash tub. Bath water was what my parents collected from rain barrels, one at each corner of the house and woodshed. In winter, my mother melted snow in the reservoir on the side of the woodstove for bathing, washing clothes. I remember I was uncomfortable at first, showering, naked, there at the school with strangers, Father Adrian looking on.

There were three boy's dorm rooms at the school. I was assigned the one for the seventh and eighth graders. There we counted off by numbers and were assigned beds, thin, hard mattresses, a pillow, woolen blanket. By this time, it was dark. I remember being hungry, having hours before eaten the bag lunch my mother had packed for the way down on the bus.

"We'll pray before you turn in," said Father Adrian.

I, a good Catholic boy, made the sign of the cross and bowed my head as he prayed.

I didn't sleep much that night. I'd never slept alone in a bed before. At home I always huddled in bed with two, and sometimes three of my brothers. My first night at St. Mary's, I remember hearing sniffles, muffled crying. I, imagining my parents, brothers, and sisters at home far away, north. I didn't cry that night, or ever, during my time there.

I don't know why. I thought of home all the time.

The bags and suitcases we'd all arrived with disappeared that first night. To the laundry, a matron had said, to be washed, stored until we went home during the holidays. My mother had washed and ironed two changes of clothes she had packed in my old suitcase, but it didn't matter. I wanted to tell the matron that, but realized it wouldn't have made a lick of difference.

We were awakened early at first light. A matron issued us two changes of underwear, socks, and tee shirts, and two uniforms each.

"Take care of them," she said. "This is all you'll be issued."

The matrons didn't talk much, I later realized. When I was older, I realized that many Native people, especially the ones raised Native, living their Native ways, don't talk a lot. They don't waste words. I imagine many of the matrons had once been students there at St. Mary's themselves, removed from their families, living in dorms only a few miles from their home community.

We were lined up and marched off to the cafeteria.

The girls had entered the cafeteria before we did and were sitting on one side of the room, many with eyes red and puffy.

"Bow your heads." One of the nuns, her voice high, shrill. She offered a blessing for the meal. I looked up and around. All the Catholics making the sign of the cross. Others, confused, not knowing what to do, having never been told to pray that way before. Having to look down to the floor, yet knowing their Creator was there, in the sky. There in the sky, beyond the stars, where they should be looking.

"Bow your heads," she said again. She walked up and down the rows, table to table, roughly pushing down heads that were not bowed, or not bowed down enough. You could see the bewildered looks on the faces of many of the young people, thinking.

"Who is this Jesus Christ she is talking about? Who is this man who died for our sins? Is this god different from *Gichi Manidoo*, our Creator? Is this god different from *Wakan Tanka*, the great mystery?"

Someone whispered, asking the one alongside them.

"Silence," she said. "We are quiet when we eat."

"English," she said. "We speak English. You will not speak your pagan tongue while you are here at St. Mary's."

Some of us began eating our oatmeal. Some too frightened to pick up our spoons, too afraid to be scolded for holding it wrong, eating too slow, or too fast.

"Eat," she said. "Clean your bowls. Thank the Lord, he has given you this food."

"Who is this lord?" I could see the confused looks on some of the other faces. Who is this lord of the oatmeal? I knew, but many didn't.

I, hungry, ate mine.

We would have oatmeal nearly every breakfast while I was there.

We would praise the Lord God, Jesus Christ. The Father, Son, the Holy Ghost.

I remember the first few nights there, some of the boys whispering to each other long after lights were out. Whispering in their language so the priest, nuns, and matrons couldn't hear them.

"Maybe the *chimookomon*, long knives, have more than one god. Maybe the *Wasi'chu* worship many gods, the father, son, the holy ghost."

Church, it seemed, was all the time. Praying before each meal, before lights out. Mass on Wednesday evenings and Sundays.

I've never been one to have a lot of friends. In elementary school in the town of Cloquet, I was one of a few reservation kids among a sea of white boys and girls. There, for the most part, I was invisible. There, I was the good Injun, adopted as the pet Indian by an occasional teacher because schooling came easy for me. Chosen by some of the white students when there was a group competition in spelling. Never invited to their homes to meet their parents, or for birthday parties, or to ride bicycles or shoot BB guns. My friends were my brothers and cousins. We were too poor to own bicycles. We didn't have BB guns. Our weapon of choice was a slingshot, carved from a maple crotch and strips of red rubber from a tire inner tube. We didn't own sleds for sliding on the hill at Pinehurst Park in Cloquet. We slid on the hills overlooking the river on the reservation. Ours sleds were cardboard or the hoods from abandoned cars. We didn't have skates, skis. We skated on the ice in our boots, walked through the woods wearing snowshoes made by our fathers, uncles.

But there at St. Mary's I was surrounded by brown faces. Boys and girls from Native communities. Sisseton, Lower and Upper Sioux, Shakopee, Prairie Island, Red Lake, White Earth, Leech Lake, Bois Forte, Mille Lacs and Grand Portage. I was, as far as I could tell, the only one from the Fond du Lac Reservation. And some of the Ojibwe boys and girls could speak the language, like me, although there were differences in ways we said certain things, dialect. Some of the Dakota boys and girls also spoke their language. These were the secret languages of our school.

I met a Dakota boy, Jay, another seventh grader, a few beds down from me in the dorm, who became my friend. He was from the Upper Sioux Agency just down the road from the school, some fifteen miles away. I can't really put a finger on why we became friends. Maybe we both finished our oatmeal when we were told. Maybe neither of us talked a lot. Maybe it was because we both had the same reservation humor. Like when one of the nuns tripped on her habit walking down the stairs of the school and fell, getting all dusty from the dirt on the floor. We both nearly peed our pants laughing once we got back in the dorms and had a chance to talk about it. Or when one of the nuns must have spilled spaghetti sauce or something on her wimple, that white collar thing they wear around their necks and head, and didn't know it, but we sure did. We laughed so hard he *booget*, farted, and I nearly had to change my underwear before we stopped. Maybe it was because both our last names started with "p," and the nuns sat us next to each other in classes in alphabetical order. Pendagayosh, Peterson, Simon, and Jay.

Now, as an old man, I think about how a long time ago our tribes, the Dakota and Ojibwe, sometimes didn't get along. We warred back and forth through what was once all Indian country, Minnesota, Wisconsin. Fighting over hunting and fishing territory, wild rice lakes, trapping areas. Fighting just for the hell of it.

"My ancestors kicked your ancestor's butts."

"No, my ancestors kicked your ancestor's butts."

So, all of a sudden it seemed, I had this Dakota friend. Teach me the Dakota word for this. Teach me the Ojibwe word for that. Tell me about your rez. No, you tell me about your rez. And as late summer turned to fall and we both seemed to enter puberty at the same time, the topics of our conversations shifted.

"Those Ojibwe girls look pretty good."

"Those Dakota girls look pretty good."

"Holaay," we'd say, almost at the same time whenever an especially pretty one walked by. That's Rez English for "not bad."

Toward the end of September, after being at St. Mary's for over a month, Father Adrian called us both into his office. We figured, of course, we were in trouble, even though neither of us had ever been in school trouble before. Maybe someone had squealed on us for laughing at one of the nuns behind their backs. Maybe someone had heard us exchanging words in our languages. Maybe this. Maybe that.

"You two boys," he began.

We both swallowed big lumps in our throats at the same time.

"You're both Catholics," he continued, "And you both were altar boys back in your communities, I understand."

"Yes, sir," One.

"Yes, sir," The other.

"My two boys from last year," he said, "they've left school. I want the two of you to fill their shoes."

Well Jesus Christ almighty, we were both thinking at the same time.

⁂

Schooling was many times easier for me than at the public school in Cloquet. Back home many of the white students were preparing for colleges or vocational schools. The high school offered advanced courses in mathematics, the sciences, English, literature, the European languages of Germany, France, Spain. At St. Mary's we had the basics. Reading, writing, mathematics, and religion. For music we learned songs from hymnals. And while the nuns would teach us to sing them in English, I would sing them in our language, in a whisper so it couldn't be heard by them or others around me. One of my favorites to this day is Amazing Grace.

Gichi-zhawenjigewining
bemaaji'igooyaan
ningagiibiingwenaaban go
noongom idash niwaab
Ningii-segiz maa ninde'ing,
ozhawenjigewining
nind-oonji-bizaaniz igo
gii-tebweyendamaan
Niibowa neniizaanak go
nimbimi-zhaabwitoon
ninga-de-dagwishimigon
owiidookaagewin
Apii gichi-gabe-ayi'ii
gii-wiijay

aawang
dibishkoo go giga-oshki-
mamiikwaanaanaan dash[4]

Many years later while living on the streets of Minneapolis when I would go to a church feeding center or shelter and the sponsors would make us pray and sing to Jesus before the meal, or before we were offered a bed, if they selected one of the songs I knew, I would sing it in our language, our beautiful language.

Still drunk but acting as sober as I could, sobering up, maybe with a buzz going, sober for a day or two, or more. There, arms high over my head, looking skyward to that place beyond the stars.

Singing, singing.

———————

Sometimes on Saturdays at the mission school we were allowed to go into town. One of the maintenance workers, a tall, skinny Dakota man, worked as bus driver as well, driving us down a dirt road into town, Granite Falls. If we were fortunate to have family that could occasionally send money, we could buy a treat while we were there. My family was large, and poor, so extra money was hard to come by. Every month, however, tucked neatly in the envelope containing long, handwritten letters from my mother was a crisp one-dollar bill. She sometimes worked as a part-time substitute nurse's aide at the Indian hospital that served our reservation. She didn't have any formal training to speak of, but changing sheets, emptying bedpans, delivering meals and playing step and fetch for the nurses and doctor didn't involve any advanced skills, she said.

I have always been frugal, able to squeeze the last juice out of a penny. While in town I'd spend a quarter for penny candy and save the rest, hiding it deep in a sock among the clothes tucked under my cot.

So, we were there in town one Saturday in October. The bus had dropped us off in the middle of downtown, the driver and Father Adrian heading off to grab cups of coffee.

"You got two hours," Father said to us.

I was just getting to know him, having been his altar boy for two weeks. I liked him. He always found a way to compliment Jay and me after mass.

"Good job," he'd say. "You two know what you're doing, and you do it well. I appreciate it."

I smiled shyly when he said those good words, of course, and look down at the floor. The nuns didn't hand out compliments, and although I wasn't looking for or expecting any, his words were good to hear.

Jay and I separated soon after we got off the bus. The school discouraged family visits, so his family always made the drive from Upper Sioux Agency into town whenever St. Mary's Mission School students made their Saturday town visits to meet up with their son. They would meet him at one of the city parks. His mother, he said, always brought some of his favorite snacks.

"I hope she brings me some *wojapi* and fry bread," he had said to me. "Do you Ojibs, his shortened word for us Ojibwe, eat *wojapi*?" he asked me.

He told me about *wojapi*, made with chokecherries. I told him my mother made chokecherry jam every fall that would be put in the larder and not opened until winter, when we would spread it on some of her homemade bread, or lug, the pan bread made with flour and baking soda.

"We call that chokecherry jam, *asasawemini-baashiminasigan*. Can you say that?" I teased.

"Chokecherry jam," he laughed.

After we parted I made my way to a five and dime variety store. I could get a lot of candy for a quarter back then, as some of it was two for a penny. A bag could last me a week or more.

I remember stepping inside the store and looking over the counter at all the penny candy. The clerk, I could tell, barely tolerated having us mission school kids in his store, the sister school, as many called it. I could always tell. Ask any person who isn't of European Caucasian descent what it feels like when they are in a store or restaurant, or any place of business for that matter that's run by white folks. Eyes are always on you, expecting you to steal something. Expecting you to browse and touch everything and not buy a thing. Expecting you to not have enough money to buy what you want, to scatter pennies, nickels, and dimes all over the counter to pay for something and still come up short.

I don't know exactly what happened, but when I was stepping back, I bumped a card rack. It tipped over with a loud crash.

The clerk raced around the counter, grabbed me by the shoulder and spun me around.

"What the hell are you trying to do, Injun?" he hollered. "You get your ass out of my store right now."

And he pushed me out the door.

⁂

There I was, standing out in the middle of the sidewalk, stunned. I just stood there for a few moments, trying to figure out what had just happened.

And then the door of the store opened and she came walking out.

"Are you okay?" She asked. Her voice, soft and low in the reservation sing-song I was so familiar with. She must have been in the store somewhere, off in a corner where I didn't notice her, all along, and was witness to everything.

"I'm okay, I guess,"

"That man," she said.

"Yes," I replied.

"What that man said was wrong," she said.

"Yes, it was," I replied.

We both just stood there on the sidewalk, eyes down, not saying anything for what seemed like the longest time. I knew she was from the sister school like me.

Silence. There is language in silence.

Then we both looked up, each of us squinting from the morning sun. "I'm Carolina," she said.

She was so beautiful. Her voice, soft, dreamy, dark, almond eyes.

"Simon," I replied. "My name is Simon."

Neither of us knowing what to say to the other. Both shy, I suppose. Me, more so. We Ojibwe have this reservation English word we use, Indianish. That means, I suppose in so many words, shy and a little backward. I guess that best describes the both of us that day.

We both turned and began walking down the sidewalk, away from the store. Away from the man who didn't like Injuns.

"Where you from?" she asked.

"*Nagachiwanong*, Fond du Lac," I replied.

"*Gaa-zagaskwaajimekaag*, Leech Lake," she replied.

"I'm in eighth grade," she said.

"I'm in seventh," I replied.

"Holaay," she said, looking me up and down. "You look older than that."

I could tell she was just teasing me.

We walked more. Found a small park and sat on a bench and talked some more. She told me all about herself, her parents and life up in Pillager country. That's what we called the people from Leech Lake. They are Pillager band. I let her talk, occasionally nodding to acknowledge I was listening just hard, as we say back on the reservation. And, of course, I'd respond on occasion.

"There's just my sister and me," she said.

"There are thirteen of us kids," I replied.

"My dad works in a lumber yard," she said.

"Mine is a logger," I replied.

"My mom is a healer," she said.

"Mine too," I replied. I didn't tell her my mother worked as an aide at the Indian hospital. Being a healer sounded better.

"I powwow," she said.

"Me too," I lied. We Catholics didn't go to powwows. Our priest forbade us from participating in the devil's work, as he called it. I'd never been to a powwow. I, a good Catholic boy, altar boy back home and now at the sister school.

"I seen you at the mass they make us go to," she said in reservation English.

"You wear that funny dress," she laughed, teasing me about the garment that altar boys wear. We Ojibwe like to tease one another. It shows we are becoming comfortable with the person we are talking with.

"I don't like showing off my shabs," I laughed. My crusty knees. I, too, becoming comfortable talking with her. We Ojibwe people are always teasing each other about body parts, crusty elbows and knees, greasy foreheads, a head way too big, no necks, no butt, having a frog body.

"I get to sip the church wine when Father Adrian isn't looking," I said to her, lying of course. "That's why I am willing to wear that dress."

She talked more than I did. I didn't have to count the words. I guess I didn't really know what to say to her. I was nervous being so close to her, she at one end of the park bench, me hugging the other end. Her voice so soft and low, so beautiful.

We talked for what seemed like the longest time. It was getting time to begin the walk back to the bus.

"We better get going, eh?" She looked toward me.

"I suppose," I replied. I, not wanting that day to end, wanting to savor it, to go on forever.

"Sko den," she said, standing, talking in perfect reservation English.

She walked ahead of me fifty feet, more or less. We knew the rules. There was no fraternizing allowed at St. Mary's. The church forbade it, the nuns said. My friend Jay and I had laughed about that rule late at night back in the dorms the day we were read the rules, including that one.

"How do you think," he laughed, "Them nuns got on this earth in the first place?"

Soon enough we got back to the bus. She climbed up into it, sat in the far back. I waited for Jay, and we got in together. I couldn't wait to tell him what happened, and about Carolina.

Once back on the bus, I whispered to him as we rumbled down the dirt road back to St. Mary's School.

"I got kicked out of a store by some crazy white guy," I said.

"Whadjudo?" he asked.

"I knocked over some stuff."

"You clumsy ass," he laughed.

"I met a girl," I said.

"You're full of it," He didn't believe me, of course.

"She's back there," I said, pointing with my lips toward the back of the bus. The back of the bus, filled with girls in all shapes and sizes.

"You're lying." He laughed.

"No, I mean it. She's right there. Her name is Carolina. She's in the eighth grade. She's that Ojibwe girl back there, the prettiest one."

"You're dreaming," he replied. "She wouldn't touch you with a ten-foot pole."

All the way back to the school, talking quietly, laughing, teasing one another back and forth. And, every once in a while, I would look back toward Carolina, to see if she was still there, still real. She, looking straight ahead, pretending not to notice me looking back toward her.

Eventually, the bus made its stop in front of the dorms and we all got out, one by one. I waited until it emptied, until Carolina made her way down the steps and stood out alongside the bus.

Then she walked toward me, slipping me a note so no one would notice as she walked by, heading for her dorm. I put it in my pocket, made my way to the boy's dorm.

There on my cot, waiting for the matron to call us for dinner, I opened it.

"Simon," it read.

"I think you're nice."

* * *

I kept the note, carried in my backpack, for years. There, preserved, wrapped in wax paper, then tinfoil, and eventually into a sandwich baggie. There, unopened most of the time, except sometimes late in evenings when the deep blue night horses ran in me.

Then one time someone stole my bag when I was living on the streets. I didn't care for anything else I'd lost that night except the pint of Thunderbird wine I was carrying.

And a yellowed piece of paper,

folded neatly

inside.

CHAPTER SIX

The Matron

Carolina

That first year at sister school I nearly didn't return when I went home for the Christmas holiday. I missed my mother and father, everything about being home from the smells in the kitchen when my mother was baking to my father's stories. I missed being around our ways. And although I would have never admitted it aloud, I missed my sister June. Those first few months at St. Mary's had been difficult, being so far from home and place.

I had slept most of the way north on the bus. We had taken a roundabout way to drop off students, making stops at the Upper and Lower Sioux communities, then north to Mille Lacs Lake. Then north again and west through Grand Rapids, Ball Club, Bena, Cass Lake, and finally Bemidji. Hours later when the bus finally pulled into the parking lot in Bemidji where the statues of Paul Bunyan and his ox stood, all I could think of was how I was going to tell my parents that I wasn't sure I want to return to that school again, that maybe I'd made a wrong choice. That it had been nothing like I had expected. That its ways were not my ways.

I remember looking out the window of the bus, iced over except for the small clearing I had scratched with my fingernails so I could peer outside, seeing my mother and father standing next to our old station wagon in the parking lot. My mother dressed in her long, dark winter coat, red hand-knitted mittens and scarf tied around her head. My father wearing his red-checkered woolen coat, soiled from years of sweat from work, cutting wood, green woolen pants, a pair of worn Redwing boots. Even now as an old woman, I remember every detail of that moment, stepping from the bus into the cold air, the packed snow crunching beneath my feet, my mother rushing to meet me, hugging me tightly. I remember the sweet smell of her. My father as well, walking to greet me, hands rough from years of hard work, cupping my face.

"My girl," his voice, gentle. In that simple greeting contained the depth of his love for me, his daughter.

"You're so quiet, Carolina," my mother said to me on the ride from Bemidji to home. Me, sitting in the back seat behind my father, not knowing what to say, so glad to be home.

Then soon enough, we pulled into the long driveway to our home, winding down the path, and then I could finally see home. There, its windows iced-over, a heavy load of snow on the roof, smoke from the wood stove coming from the chimney. My sister June, soon to be returning home from Auntie's, who was taking care of her while my parents retrieved me from the bus.

I remember stepping from the car, the air cold, crisp, the smell of woodsmoke. My father, carrying my suitcase. My mother, brooming off a thin layer of new snow off the porch before we entered. I remember stepping inside and being overwhelmed by the smells. My mother had been baking, readying for Christmas. For even though we were not Christians, we celebrated Christmas. We had a tree my father cut from the bush, and when I was younger, I remember going out with him, he, carrying a bow saw and hand ax, searching to find the best tree. We exchanged presents, always something hand-made. Mittens, a cap, a pair of knitted stockings, a monkey sock doll, a sock full of nuts, candies. And things that were used would disappear days before Christmas day, only to find themselves under the tree on Christmas day. Old stockings, darned. A doll, missing an eye, with a new button to replace it. I remember rubbing my father's boots and moose-hide choppers with bear grease on Christmas eve, wrapping them in brown paper and tying them up with string, and placing them under the tree for Christmas morning.

I, quiet, following my mother around the kitchen while she prepared dinner. My father out in the woodshed, splitting firewood to last the next few days. My sister June, who had returned home soon after we did, in her room, playing.

"You're so quiet, my girl," she said, again. "Is something wrong?"

Then I, standing there, arms down by my sides, there in the kitchen wearing one of her aprons that she had me wear so I could help her.

A tear. My lower lip, quivering.

"*Ni-maama*, my mother," I, now crying.

Then she, setting her work aside, moving pans filled with boiling potatoes and wild rice away from the hot burners of the kitchen stove, taking me in her arms and leading me to the couch, sitting down beside me.

"My girl," she said.

"It's okay, my girl," she said. "It's going to be okay now."

"You're home now."

"You're home now."

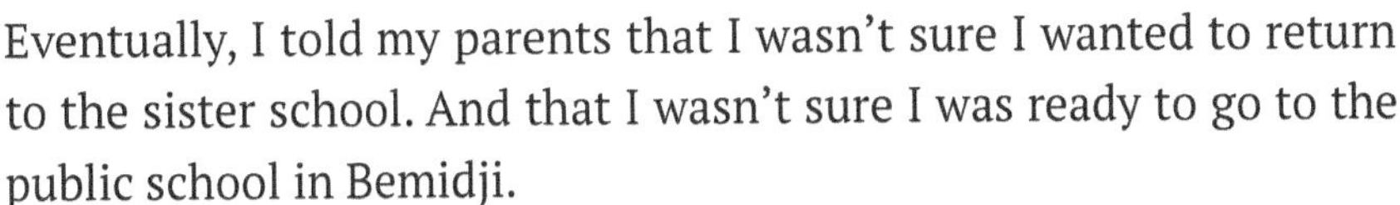

Eventually, I told my parents that I wasn't sure I wanted to return to the sister school. And that I wasn't sure I was ready to go to the public school in Bemidji.

"You miss home," my father said.

"I do,"

"You miss me," I heard my little sister June shout from our room, where she had been sent while my parents talked with me.

"No, I don't miss you," I said in return. There was a hint of truth in what I said.

"You miss my cooking," My mother.

A slight smile from me, looking down at the floor.

"What is it, my girl?" My mother.

"It's just . . . so different there."

"Tell us."

So, I told them. The dorms. Being in a room with fifty other girls. The nuns. I don't think they like young people. They can be pretty mean. The priest. The priest and nuns look scary the way they are dressed in black, their habits and robes. The food isn't nearly as good as here at home.

"Not. Even. Close." I said to emphasize it.

"Have you found friends?" My mother.

"I do. I have found friends. They're from all the different reservations." I smiled slightly.

"However," I continued.

"They don't allow us to speak our language. I mean, we can speak it, but not when they are around. And they make us go to their church, and to pray all the time. We're not Catholic. I'm not Catholic. There in that church. We stand, we kneel, we stand, kneel, over and over again. They sing these songs I don't know the meaning to. The priest talks in a language I don't understand."

My mother spoke then.

"Their ways," she said. "Their ways are different from ours. The way they talk to the Creator is different than ours. The way they sing is different. They speak in Latin, the language of their church. I know. I know, when I was sent to their school when I was young it was like that as well. Then, it was different. We were beaten for speaking our language. We were forced to learn their ways, their prayers and songs. We were told our ways were of the devil."

"One of the nuns said our language was the devil's tongue," I said.

"And do you believe what she said is true?" She replied.

"No, I don't believe that."

"They believe," she said. "That their way is the only way. That all others are wrong. I am not saying I believe we are right and they are wrong. It could very well be their Jesus is the son of the Creator. From all that I have heard and read maybe he was. And maybe there is a heaven and a hell. I just know in our ways we speak of that place beyond the stars. When I first heard about their heaven it sounded a lot like what our teachers describe, that place we will travel to some day on our westward journey. Maybe our hell is here, all the suffering we sometimes see in people, around the world all the suffering, the starvation and drought, earthquakes. Maybe when we suffer, we experience hell. The evil, the devil they speak of, we also believe that everything has an opposite and an equal. Evil exists. But is it a devil? I don't know. We sometimes refer to that spirit that whispers in our ears to do bad things as the Other. But to us, the Other is not a devil. It just is. It is that opposite voice that speaks to us. So, I just know that evil exists as well as good.

"I just know, my girl," She continued. "There is more than one path to the Truth. And that Truth is our Creator. I know when they talk about their god and their Jesus, that is their way of honoring the Creator. I just know the Creator they speak of is the same one we pray to, the same one we are making offerings to, sing to."

Both my mother and father had a way of explaining things, of speaking in such a way that made sense to me.

"Does any of what I have told you make any sense, my girl?" She said to me.

I nodded, acknowledging her words. I loved my mother and father so much. Even now, me an old woman, I remember their words as clearly as they spoke them like it was yesterday. Both who could say things with so much meaning in so few words.

When the bus returned to pick up students several weeks later, I was there to meet it. I had made friends there. The school was small and all my fellow classmates were Native, brown like me. I could speak my language, albeit behind the backs of the nuns, priest, and matrons. I could bear to hear the words and songs of their way of worshipping knowing it was their way, but not mine. That in my mother's words, there are many paths to the Truth, there is no one way. That our ceremonies were our way, as good or better than any other.

So, I returned to St. Mary's Mission, the sister school, that year of my seventh grade. And when I returned home in the spring, I knew that come fall as well. I would gather together with other students in Bemidji to take the bus south again.

I filled the summer before my second year at St. Mary's to overflowing with all of the things I missed while at school. My mother and I sewed a new dance outfit for me of blue satin, representing the earth and sky, trimmed with ribbons. Red for the dawn, the eastern sky, yellow, black, and white ribbons in the colors of the directions. She had been teaching me applique beadwork, and on the back of my shawl I beaded a yellow star, my Ojibwe name, *Anung*, Star.

We went to every powwow we could. I danced every dance possible. In the competition dances at Red Lake and Ball Club I won the girl's fancy shawl dance category, and the prize money was saved for school, stashed away in my suitcase for my return south. We harvested birchbark from the bush, made baskets and sold them. I helped my father flesh deer hide for tanning to make moccasins. We went to summer ceremonies, camped in a tent for four days, sat in the teaching lodge and listened as our teachers talked story long into the evenings. Stories about the earth and sky and all the spirits that dwell there. Stories of our creation and migrations, our wars, of the good times and hard times. And each one bearing lessons about how we should live, and continue to practice our ways. I, just becoming a young woman, knowing the importance of listening to every story, learning it, knowing the day would come when it would be my time to lead the talk, sitting there in the lodge doing our crafts, keeping our hands busy, our minds open.

That summer I would follow my mother deep into the bush as she gathered the plants used for her medicines, where she would sing for each one, offer them *asemaa*, tobacco, say prayers to the spirits of the plants, and to our Creator.

"My girl," She would say. "Do you know the songs for this plant, the prayers?"

And I would reply, "I do. I remember them."

"You need to know each one," She would remind me.

"I will," I would reply.

"Someday," she would say. "I will be too old to come out here. You will need to come here by yourself, or with one of your children, and gather them for me.

And someday, when I am no longer here you will go in the bush and do all of the things that need to be done so there will always be someone who knows the medicines, to harvest them, dry, make the poultices, teas."

That summer, as well, I spent many evenings with my Aunties and they reminded me of the responsibilities of being a woman. They said that someday I would meet a man and that I would fall in love. That someday I would bear children and raise them, the man and I. That I would teach them all that I know.

"Auntie," I remember asking. "How will I know this man?"
"You will know," Each one laughed.
"You will know."

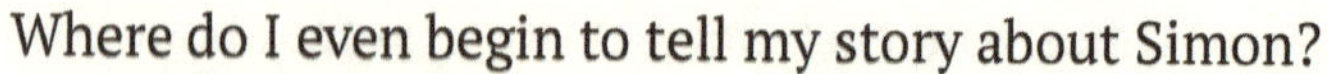

Where do I even begin to tell my story about Simon?

It was a Saturday in early October of my second year at the sister school and we had taken the school's bus into town, Granite Falls. Normally on such days, I would have gone off to browse the stores with my girlfriends. We liked to window shop the clothing stores, finger the goods in the cosmetics section, wishing our way through the eyeliner, lipstick, makeup we were not allowed to wear.

That day, though, I decided to go off on my own, and the first place I stopped was a variety store. I was back in a corner, looking at barrettes, when he walked in. I could tell what he wanted, as he went straightaway for the candy. And I could tell he was from the sister school. He just had that look about him. It didn't take him long to get into trouble, when he caused this big commotion knocking over the greeting cards.

He didn't even get a chance to say he was sorry. That man in the store grabbed him and marched him right out the door, hollering hurtful words as he did. I'd heard them words before and knew their meaning. The rare times at my old school, when one of the white boys dared say anything bad about us Native kids.

I quietly left the store shortly after that, trying to be invisible, to not become another victim of the storekeeper's wrath. And outside, standing in the middle of the sidewalk, squinting in the bright sun, was the boy. I said something to him in English, to help him not feel so bad, and when he answered, I knew by the tone and cadence in his voice that he was Ojibwe like me. We have this way we talk sometimes. In today's language, we might say he sounded really rezzy.

"*Aniin ezhi-nikaazoyan?*" I asked him then in our language. What is your name?

"Simon Pendagayosh, *nindizhinakaaz*," He responded. My name is Simon Pendagayosh.

We talked more then, in the language, as we walked down the street. Soon enough we settled into a bench in a nearby park, and talked some more. I talked more than he, I know I did. He, shy, I think, or nervous, or both.

We talked until it was time to return to the bus. I got up to leave first, kept my pace to remain far enough ahead of him so the priest wouldn't become suspicious that we had spent most of our time in town together. Fraternizing with persons of the opposite sex was strictly forbidden, punishable with confinement to the dorms, extra chores cleaning latrines and toilets.

All the way back to school that day I had to pretend I didn't know him. More than once, I noticed he was looking back at me. I was good at it, keeping my eyes looking straight ahead at the back of the head of the bus driver. Before we all got off the bus upon our return, I wrote him a note on a scrap of paper and passed it on to him as I walked by him on my way to the girl's dorm.

Months later he told me he was keeping the note forever as a keepsake.

"Why?" I asked.

"Because."

"Because why?"

"Because it will forever be a reminder to me of you."

After that day, we tried to get together whenever we could. In the cafeteria we would look across the room into each other's eyes, hoping none of the nuns or matrons would notice. Passing each other on our way to the dorms and classrooms, we would slow down just enough to look into each other's eyes and mutter a greeting. And on the Saturdays when we were allowed to go into town, we would meet, secretly, out in the middle of one of the town parks, hidden away among the trees, away from any students who might tell a matron, or a nun, or Father Adrian. There, together on those Saturday trips to Granite Falls, we would talk, sharing our stories about home, school, and what we wanted to do with our lives.

And when that was not enough, we pledged that we would sneak out of our dorms one night a week and meet up, late in the evening when we knew the matrons watching over us would be long asleep. There, through bitterly cold winter nights, or when it was snowing, during all the phases of the moon, we would meet. There, in the field behind the girl's dorm.

There, talking in whispers.

I remember our first kiss. I think he wasn't expecting it, but when he began to turn his head away, expecting I would kiss him on the cheek, I touched his face with my hand and turned him to meet my lips.

"We'd better go in," I said.

"Yes, I think so."

Then we would meet again the following week out there in the field, out where the grasses met the edge of the cottonwood trees. And during the days we could only fleetingly acknowledge each other as we passed each other in the school yard or the cafeteria, or in the hallways of the school, we would look that certain way into each other's eyes, if only for a brief moment, that way two people do when they are falling in love.

This went on for months. The spirit of fall succumbed to the spirit of winter, which fought fiercely yet finally retreated to the sky to the spirit of spring. The first buds on the cottonwood trees, daffodils, the smell of new grass sprouting, pushing its way up through the earth, the sound of peepers in the creek that ran out behind the school. There, on late evenings one day a week,

Simon and I. Sitting in the grass, facing one another, holding each other's hands.

Now as an old woman looking back to that time in all its innocence. I, then just a young woman, keenly aware of the teachings of my mother and aunties of my responsibility to save myself for marriage. Simon, innocent himself, respectful of me, maybe too shy and hesitant, maybe too ignorant to know what to do. I will never know. Still, it was love. I cannot lessen or deny it was, that young love is entirely possible, indeed. That if Juliet, just thirteen years of age, and Romeo, at just sixteen years, could have such a love, we could as well.

That it was as real as anything I have experienced the whole of my lifetime.

⟶

I remember it was the first week in May 1957. I, just fourteen years old, my body blossoming into that of a woman, but still a child in many ways. Simon and I had been seeing each other every other week when we were allowed to go to town, and weekly at our arranged time and place, out behind the girl's dorms. There at the cleave of the field and cottonwoods.

Realizing in just three weeks we would be going our separate ways for the summer, wanting to make our short visits last.

I had been telling him about the medicine work my mother was teaching me, the different plants. I remember picking a dandelion, a plant that seemingly can grow anywhere there is sunlight, telling him how we used the petals, among many other things, as medicine for the liver and gallbladder, the leaves to help with the kidneys. Then I picked some squirrel tail, and gave it to him.

"Chew this," I said. He did, and told me it tasted awful.

"When you need to treat a cut or a bee sting, you pick these and chew them. Put it on the cut or sting bite. It will stop the bleeding from a cut, ease the pain, heal the bite.

My mother has been teaching me that there are healing plants everywhere. There are hundreds of them, many of them right here around us now. That is what I will do when I grow up. I'll be a healer like my mother."

Simon told me about playing lacrosse and the skill involved in making lacrosse sticks, a skill he had only watched but wanted to master someday. He told me about the rugged games he played with his brothers and cousins through the woods, fields, and swamps near his home.

"When I get home this summer, I can't wait to play a game," he said. "I think I'm pretty good at it. I want to be as good as my older brothers."

And he told me about running dogs, describing his dogs, Jake, Asker, and LaVern and dogsledding, riding with his father through the trails.

"I've missed my dogs," he said. And although he didn't say it, I knew he was also saying he missed his father as well.

"Is that what you want to do when you grow up?" I asked.

"Oh, for sure. And I want my kids to play lacrosse and run dogs, too."

Then he was quiet for a while, but finally spoke. "But I really want to be a writer. I want to write books."

"Books? What kind of books?"

"If I say you might laugh at me."

"Come on. Tell me."

"No."

"Oh, come on. Tell me."

He hesitated, twirling a dandelion in his hand. "I want to write a poetry book."

"Poetry. That's so sweet, Simon."

"Tell me one of your poems, Simon."

"No way."

Oh, come on. Tell me."

"Nope."

That is as far as I got.

Then he pulled something from under his coat.

"Something to remember me by this summer," he said.

From his coat emerged a flute. A flute he had made of the sumac that grew at the edge of the field behind the girl's dorm, made by hand with a pen knife he secretly kept hidden under his mattress.

"Here," he said, handing it to me. "I made this for you. Try it out. Be quiet though."

It had five holes. I put it to my mouth, blew into it. Put my fingers over each of the holes, trying each note. There, in the field behind the girl's dorm, blowing softly on the flute he had made for me. There, the sound so sweet and beautiful, mingling with the music of the peepers in the creek that flowed down by the cottonwoods.

"Simon, it's beautiful." I kissed him on the cheek.

"My uncle taught me how to make them," he said.

Later when I made my way back to my dorm room, I carefully wrapped the flute into a piece of cloth and put it in my suitcase under the bed, planning on bringing it home with me.

It wasn't until I was in university some years later in an American Indian Studies class, Native American Music, that I would learn the flute was used by young men to court a love interest in our ancient villages. That they would sit somewhere within hearing range of the girl's wigwam and play the love flute.

Young Simon, a romantic, poet, a flutist.

Several evenings later, an hour or more after lights out, I was awakened by a matron.

"Carolina," she whispered. "Get dressed and come with me."

I, still in a sleepy fog, slowly got dressed while she waited for me, then followed her out the door, quietly so we would not awaken others. I remember it was chilly and damp that evening, dark, without a moon.

We walked across the yard, past the school building toward the church. There to a side door in the back, she opened it and stood aside.

"You go in there, the sacristy," she said. I still remember the sound of her voice, sweet and low in the sing-song of the old-time Native people.

The door closed behind me. The room, dimly light, a yellowing light bulb overhead.

Why am I here, I was thinking? What could be wrong? All these thoughts racing through my head.

A voice. Father Adrian.

"Carolina, come here."

Father Adrian, standing over where his vestments and those of the altar boys hung. I approached slowly. I don't think I could recall the priest ever speaking to me before, let alone knowing me by name.

"Carolina," he said. "Sit down," pointing to a chair.

"Father," I remember saying, "Is something wrong? Have I done something wrong?"

Silence for what seemed like the longest time. Then he finally spoke.

"Carolina," he said. "You have been seeing a boy, Simon, one of my altar boys. Is that true?"

My hands were folded, fingering the hem of my dress. Eyes looking downward toward the floor. I, almost ready to cry, knowing now that we had been discovered.

"Father," I said, my voice trembling.

"Father, we just talk. That's all."

"From what I hear, it is much more than talk, Carolina."

Silence.

"Carolina, you are well aware of our rules against fraternizing?"

Tears began to flow, run down my cheeks, slowly falling onto my dress.

"Are you having relations with Simon?"

"No, father."

"Why should I believe you?"

"Come here, Carolina."

I, sitting there, too frightened to move.

"Come here, Carolina," he said again with more authority.

Me, crying softly now.

He came walking toward me. Touching me.

I remember then, his hands. One hand over my mouth, the other finding its way under my dress. I, sobbing, protesting. The rough stubble of the hair on his face against me. His breath, hot. My body, frozen with fear.

What he did to me.

When he was done with me, he told me to get dressed. My dress, buttons ripped, picking it up off the floor and putting it on, sobbing.

"Carolina," I remember him saying. "You will not speak a word of this. No one will believe you. Do you hear me? No one will believe you."

Then I, backing slowly toward the door, reaching for the doorknob and slowly turning it. It opened and I stepped out into the night. And there, at the corner of the back of the church, just outside the door, standing only a few feet from me. There in the darkness.

The matron.

The matron, whose soothing voice had awakened me that night, the cadence and sing-song of her words reminding me of the old time Native people, of my aunties. The one who had called me to come with her that night. To come with her to see the priest.

There, her eyes cast downward, dutifully waiting, hands folded neatly at her waist

as if

in prayer.

CHAPTER SEVEN

The Long Journey Home

Simon

Every day, or nearly so, since Carolina and I had met outside the store while on one of our Saturday trips to Granite Falls, we had seen and at least, acknowledged one another. So, when she wasn't in the cafeteria one morning, or passing in the halls at school or in the yard, I wondered about her. Morning passed, afternoon, and after dinner I asked one of her classmates as we were filing out of the cafeteria if they knew where she was.

"Have you seen Carolina Shaugobay today?"

"I heard she is not feeling well. She's staying in the dorm." The reply.

The following day she wasn't in the cafeteria, school, passing in the yard. So, I asked her classmate again.

"Is Carolina still sick? Is she okay?"

"She is. She was still in bed when we left the dorm this morning, and when I was there just before dinner." The reply. "I went over to her cot and she was all covered up, even her face. I said to her,

'Carolina, are you feeling alright? I hope you get better soon. Simon has been asking about you.' I was teasing her a little bit, you know, about you."

"Simon," she asked, smiling coyly, "Is there something going on between Carolina and you?"

"We're just friends," I replied, mumbling my words, lying. There at the school, one didn't know who could or couldn't be trusted, who might say something to a matron, nun, the priest. There were rules, and sometimes even fellow students were part of their enforcement. There were always some who were currying favor from a nun, or the priest.

That second night Carolina and I had previously made plans to meet out in the field behind the girl's dorm. I always waited, lying in my cot until nearly midnight, until I quietly got up, pretending I was going to use the bathroom, but instead making my way out the door. Hugging the side of the buildings until I came to the girl's dorm, then going to the back, to the field.

There I sat in the grass, waiting. Waiting to see if Carolina would come to me. I remember the night was clear, and the stars shone in all their beauty. Peepers and crickets chirping down by the creek. A gentle wind rustling the grasses, the cottonwoods black in the darkness. And I waited for what seemed like the longest time.

An hour passed. And another.

In time, I realized she wasn't coming out to meet me.

Sometimes, I think, we have a sense about things, that sense our animal relatives were gifted with. I know now we humans have it as well, most of us anyway, we just don't practice using it. We don't call it out. I learned to call it out, that sense, later as an adult, when I was living on the streets. Some call it that, street sense.

That night long ago, when I returned back to the dorm, I lay in my cot for the longest time before I was able to sleep. And in morning when the matron rang the wakeup bell, I slept through it, and she had to awaken me.

"Simon," she shook me. "Simon Pendagayosh, you get up, right now."

I, groggy, sleepy all day. Worried. That sense strong in me that something was wrong.

"The matron said that Carolina is still ill," her classmate offered to me as we passed in the school halls. I didn't even have to ask about her whereabouts.

Come near midnight I made my way outside again. Maybe she would show this evening, I was thinking. Maybe she is getting well enough to leave her bed. Maybe she knows I am worried about her. I remember rounding the corner of the girl's dorm, out to the back of the field where we always met. Back by the cleave of the field and Cottonwoods.

And there, sitting in the grass, was Carolina.

I bent down to kiss her, but she turned her head away, my lips brushing the side of her head, her hair. Then I sat in the grass beside her and took her hand.

"Carolina, are you feeling alright?"

She didn't respond. I could see she was looking down toward the ground.

"Carolina, is something wrong?"

I leaned over and turned her face to me with both of my hands, kissing her softly. My hands felt the warm, wet of her tears.

"Carolina, please. Please tell me what's wrong."

She remained quiet.

Some Native people still recognize the language in silence. Nowadays, I suppose, there are fewer of us who were raised in that way, who still know this. We have more of our own people, growing in numbers with each passing generation, it seems, who seem to have lost the ability to recognize the language in pauses, silence. Too many of us now, especially the young and in those who may be Native but not raised in that way, unfortunately, seem to need to fill a void with words. To chatter away meaninglessly.

I sitting there with Carolina that late evening, holding her hand, her head hung, crying softly.

Every once in a while, I would squeeze her hand, letting her know I was there, waiting. And I would reach over with my other hand and gently touch her face, and wipe her tears away.

We, sitting there in the cool grass that early spring evening so many years ago.

"Carolina," I whispered, "when you are ready, okay? You can tell me what is wrong."

She buried her head into my chest then, still sobbing quietly. My hand stroking her hair, rocking her back and forth.

Finally, after many minutes, she spoke, quietly.

"Simon . . ." Hesitantly.

"Simon . . . I love you Simon . . . I love you," she said.

Now as an old man, I still remember her words from that evening many years ago.

"I love you, Carolina," I replied. "I love you."

The first time either of us had said those words to each other. We held each other for the longest time and kissed. Finally, she wiped the tears away from her face.

"Simon," she said. "I have something to tell you."

"When you are ready," I replied.

"I have something to tell you," She repeated softly.

And then, she told me.

<hr>

All of those months in school, Father Adrian had catered to me. I, one of his altar boys. I, a good Catholic boy, knowing every move he required of me in the ritual Catholic mass, replying to his incantations of Latin, the timing of each genuflection, the passing of the Eucharistic bread and wine, the proper way to hold the robe of his vestments when he would walk down the aisle of the church, blessing the nuns, matrons, girls, and boys with holy water, or incense.

Father Adrian, who would sometimes smile and pat the top of my head like I was some kind of pet. I, craving the positive attention. Now I, my eyes black with rage looking in the direction of the rectory, where Father Adrian surely was fast asleep.

"Carolina," I said, my voice shaking. "I want you to go back into your dorm and get a change of clothes. A coat too. We need to leave here."

"Do you have any money?" I asked. She shook her head that she did.

"That as well," I told her.

"I'm going to go get clean clothes as well," I continued. "I only have a few dollars."

"I'll meet you back here, right here, okay? In fifteen minutes." I said to her.

I helped her up.

We parted at the corner of the girl's dorm. My eyes on the rectory. Then slowly, quietly, hugging the sides and corners of the school, the church. I climbed the steps of his residence and tried the door. Unlocked.

Quietly, entering, letting my eyes adjust to the darkness. Then slowly making my way across the living and dining room. Ready to ask him, confront him, why. The anger and betrayal so strong in me.

His bedroom door open, I peered in. The bed, empty.

Where was he, I was thinking, so late in the evening?

So, I walked back to the door. Resting against the trim, a walking stick he sometimes used when crossing the yard, and when we went into town on Saturdays. I picked it up. It was heavy, a hardwood. Stepping out into the night air, I noticed the church was dimly lit. Slowly making my way there. Opening the door silently, carefully, so I wouldn't be heard. The church lit by two candles on the altar.

And there he was, kneeling in prayer, Father Adrian. Praying softly from the rite of penance, over and over again,

Lord Jesus, Son of God,
have mercy on me, a sinner.

It was all surreal.

"Father," I said, breaking the cadence of his incantations. He turned his head toward me, still kneeling.

"Father," I said as I swung the stick in rage to his head, back, over and over again.

He, lying unconscious near the altar, before the statue of Jesus on the cross. Blood coming from his head, ears.

And I, turning away, speaking.

"This is for what you did," I said.

"This is for what you did to Carolina."

I made my way back to my dorm, entering quietly, put on a change of clothes and retrieved the money I had, three dollars. Then I went a few beds down to my friend Jay's cot.

"Jay," I whispered into his ear. "Jay, wake up."

I shook him.

"Jay, wake up."

He awakened slowly, opening his eyes.

"Hey," he whispered.

"Jay, I have to leave here. Carolina and I."

"What? Why? Where are you going?"

"I don't know. We just have to leave. Now. Jay, do you have any money you can lend me?"

He sat up, groggily.

"Lemme see," he said, searching under his pillow where he hid his money every night, away from the thieves that seem to be everywhere.

"I got four bucks, Simon. Here."

"I'll pay you back. I promise," I said, taking the money and stuffing it into my pants pocket.

"Why do you have to leave?" He asked again. "Where are you going?"

"We have to leave this place, now. I'll see you again," I whispered, uttering one of the few Dakota words he had taught me. "Thank you, *koda*, friend."

"Simon," he said. "Go to Upper Sioux Agency, my community. There will be people who will help you there. Help you get home."

Carolina was there at our meeting spot as planned. I did not tell her what I had just done.

Then we were gone.

Many years later when I was living on the streets, I made my way to the Minneapolis Indian Center during a sober streak for one of those free community feasts. Me there, in many days worn jeans and a stretched-out sweater I'd found digging through the free boxes at St. Vincent de Paul's. Then those of us sitting at the same table got around to introducing ourselves, and someone asked me to start first.

"Simon," I said. "Simon Pendagayosh."

There was an older gentleman there, a Dakota man, along with his wife.

"Simon," he said, a smile so wide it took up most of his face. "Simon, do you remember me? Jay, we met many years ago at St. Mary's? Jay Peterson."

He reached across the table and I took his hand.

"How are you?" He asked.

"What have you been up to all these years?"

All the things I wanted to not say. I've been drunk for years now. Sometimes living in shelters and on the street. Sometimes in a rooming house.

Lost, that's where I've been. Wounded.

Running. Still running away from that school, that place.

From life.

"I'm doing fine," I replied.

"I'm doing just fine."

"And you?" I asked.

"Fine. I'm doing just fine."

Later, he made his way to me alone, just as I was leaving.

"Simon," he said. "I was always wondering what became of you. I'm glad you made it home alright."

I nodded in acknowledgement to him, but I never really made it home, I wanted to say. Not really.

"Simon?" he asked.

"Whatever became of Carolina?"

━━━━✦━━━━

Dark, running from that school, from what happened there.

We walked for miles, following the road signs heading toward Granite Falls.

"Where are we going?" Carolina asked.

"We'll get to Marshall," I replied, a larger town some thirty miles southwest that certainly must have a bus depot. "We'll get to a bus station there and take a bus home. How much money did you say you have?"

"Twenty dollars," she replied. "My powwow winnings."

We had twenty-seven dollars between us. I hoped it was enough for two bus tickets. My plan, decided without much forethought. Walking until first light on the dirt road heading toward Granite Falls. There was no traffic.

We left the road for a grove of trees come sunrise. Huddling together to keep each other warm, we slept on the cool ground. After several hours I awakened her. We had a long way to go, I said. We need to get to the bus station, leave as soon as we can before they find us.

We walked more, hiding in ditches whenever a car came along. There weren't many. Then off in the distance, Granite Falls. We skirted the town, avoiding being seen, continuing south. Eventually we came to a junction to a road headed east, a sign that read, "Upper Sioux Agency five miles." We sat on the upper side of the ditch, resting for a while. Then we started on our way again.

We had made it no more than a few hundred feet when a car approached, came to a stop at the stop sign. It was an older vehicle, rusty, loud, like maybe it had a hole in the muffler. It must be a rez car, a war pony, I was thinking. We didn't have time to hide in the field. It pulled out, heading our way, and pulled to a stop alongside us.

The side window rolled down, a Native woman. I could see inside. A man driving and four little kids sitting in the back seat.

"Where you going?" she said with a thick reservation English accent. "You need a ride?"

I nodded in acknowledgement that we, indeed, could use a ride.

"Get in then."

We climbed into the backseat. Two of the kids climbed onto our laps.

"Where you going?" The man asked.

"Marshall," I replied. "We're going to the bus station. How far are you going?"

"We're going to Sioux Falls," he said. "There's a powwow there."

"You two are pretty young to be traveling all by yourselves," the woman said.

"We're from the school," I said. "We're going home."

"We figured that," she said. "We'll take you to Marshall. It's on our way."

Neither of the adults asked us why we were running from the school. It wasn't unusual for students to run from there. For most, the school was a long way from family and their communities. Loneliness was most often the reason for leaving. Every month a few would leave. Most would return a day or two later, tired and hungry. Some we would never see again. The school would send the maintenance man, bus driver, out in search of any missing ones. Many times, he found them, some of the time not. The ones that returned we would see in the dorms, confined there for four or five days as punishment, fed oatmeal.

Off we went down Highway 23 toward Marshall. The woman, the children's mother, soon passed a greasy brown paper bag in back to Carolina.

"You kids must be hungry," she said. "Have some fry bread."

Then she passed a half-gallon jug of tea back as well, saying, "and thirsty, too."

We each took a piece, chewing it hungrily, passing the bag to the little kids sitting on our laps. We each took large swallows of the warm, sweet tea, and passed the jug to the little kids as well.

"Where you kids from?" the man asked. We told him.

"Holaay, you're a long way from home," his reply. "You must miss home."

Neither of us replied, although we both did miss our parents and other relatives a great deal. I didn't say anything about the deep trouble I was in. That by now, I was sure, the police were looking for me.

In about a half hour we were pulling into Marshall, and soon thereafter we pulled onto a side street downtown.

"There's the bus station there," the woman turned and said to us. "You kids have enough money for tickets?"

"I don't know. I hope so," My reply.

"Lemme come in with you two," she said. "They might not want to sell you tickets knowing you're both Native and probably figuring you are running away from somewhere. Give me some of that fry bread," she said to a kid in the back seat, the one holding the greasy bag.

"Here," she said, handing us each a large piece. "Put those in your coat pockets. Yous two will get hungry on your ways home."

We got out of the car with the woman and walked into the bus depot. Along the way, she asked us where we were going.

"Bemidji," I said. Carolina remained quiet. I, it seemed was doing all the talking for both of us.

"Gimme your money," she said to us. We dug in our pockets and gave her the crumpled paper bills we each had.

She went up to the counter and bought two one-way tickets, and returned to us, handing them to us and some change. Then, she dug into her coin purse and gave us a dollar each.

"Here," she said. "You might need some extra for something."

Then she took Carolina by the hand, and put her other hand on my shoulder, speaking to us quietly, gently.

"Yous are going to have to transfer in Minneapolis," she said. "You stay there in the bus depot when you get there. Don't go out onto the streets."

"Be safe," she said. "Be safe."

And then she was gone.

⁘

We sat, waiting in the bus depot for several hours. It finally arrived just after noon and we climbed aboard, handing our tickets to the driver, who punched and gave them back to us. We retreated somewhere near the back to seats.

Then we were off.

We made stops along the way to Minneapolis, it seemed, in every small town. Sometimes at gas stations and wayside restaurants. Redwood Falls, Morton, Hector, Stewart, Brownton, Gencoe, Cologne, Chaska, then north more miles into downtown Minneapolis.

Carolina, quiet, talking little, except to ask me every once in a while.

"Simon, we're going home to where I'm from, my home. How are you going to get home? I don't even know if there's a bus going to Fond du Lac Rez from Bemidji."

"Don't worry about me," I replied. "I'll figure it out. I just want to make sure you make it home alright. Safe."

I, acting like a man, being the protector.

When we arrived into the Minneapolis station, we heeded the words of the Dakota woman to stay in the station. It was nearly four in the afternoon when we arrived. The bus to Bemidji wouldn't be leaving for nearly two hours. We wouldn't arrive into Bemidji until nearly midnight. Sitting in the bus station, nibbling on our fry bread. I bought a bottle of orange soda we shared. Then finally, our bus was called over the intercom.

North, stopping at all the little towns along the way. Sunset came just after eight in the evening. Darkness fell, and Carolina slept, her head resting on my shoulder. I sat there awake, stroking her hair, knowing when we arrived, we must part and that I might not see her for a long time, maybe forever. Knowing the police would eventually catch up to me.

Then, nearing midnight we arrived at the bus station in Bemidji. Tired, we stepped off the bus. It was cold. We stood there on the side-walk, wrapping our coats around us.

"My home is this way," Carolina said to me, pointing south and east with her lips.

We walked all night, first through the backstreets of Bemidji, then down Old Cass Lake Highway. Whenever we saw approaching head-lights off in the distance we would hide in the fields, or woods, fear-ing it might be the police.

"They might send us back," I said to Carolina.

Finally, as dawn approached, we rounded a corner and crossed the second bridge over the Mississippi River, it being only forty or so feet across that far north, less than an hour's drive from its source, its beginning. Carolina said we were less than a mile from her home.

We rounded another corner, then she stopped in front of a driveway that led out into the bush. A mailbox, reading "Shaugobay."

"We're here," she said, smiling slightly for the first time since she told me what had happened to her.

"I'm home," she said, hugging me tightly.

"Thank you so much, Simon," she said, tears in her eyes. "For getting me home."

We held each other for the longest time, kissing.

Then, slowly, eventually, I broke free.

"I need to go," I said.

"No," she said. "You come with me. My parents will figure out a way to get you home."

"No," I said. "I can't. It wouldn't be appropriate for them to know we have made our way here, just the two of us. No, you go home now. I'll be alright, Carolina. I'll make it home."

"No . . ." she pleaded. "Simon . . ."

She tried to hold me, keep me there.

"Carolina, you're home now," I said. "You need to go home now."

I turned and began walking away, and she, standing there at the end of her driveway, watching me. Me, turning around and watching her standing there, waiting for her to disappear down her drive. Then, a corner, I stopped and waved back to her.

"Carolina," I yelled. "I love you. I love you."

Carolina

My parents were both up when I walked in the door, having coffee. The house was nice and warm, a fire going in the woodstove to take the chill out.

"My girl," my mother called out, running to me, holding me. My father walked to me, hugging both my mother and me at the same time. I could see both of their faces, tears welled up in their eyes.

"Baby girl," my mother said, crying.

My father had to go to work, but later that afternoon when he returned, he sat me down and I told him about missing home too much.

"How did you get here?" He asked.

"By bus," I replied back to him.

"Where did you get the money?" He asked.

"Powwow winnings," I said with a half-smile.

As soon as he left, and my mother got my sister June off to school, she sat me down on the couch and we had a long talk.

"I'm never going back there," I told her firmly.

Neither my mother or father ever found out what happened to me at St. Mary's, about what Father Adrian had done to me. I kept that secret, hidden from them, throughout the rest of their lifetimes. And I never shared it with anyone else, including my sister June, until I was much older, until it burst out of me one late night many years later, there at ceremonies, in the lodge where we, the old women were sitting around the fire, talking story.

And where, upon hearing my story, all encircled and held me, cried with me, long into the night.

"Oh, my girl," Each of them saying, consoling me. "My girl."

These things we carry.

Simon

I walked several miles from Carolina's driveway to Highway Two, the main highway going southeast toward home, some one hundred twenty-five miles away. Along the way wondering when or if I would ever see Carolina again. Wondering if I had killed Father Adrian for what he had done to her. Wondering what I would tell my father and mother. I remember it was early morning, still and cool, ground fog in the fields, crows talking as they quietly flew low above me. I could hear the sounds of their wings as they came over the trees, then disappeared. The occasional bark of a dog.

All I had on me was some pocket change, not anywhere near enough to buy a bus ticket. I'd have to rely on the goodwill of others, stick out my thumb and see who might pick me up. There I stood, on the side of the road for an hour or more, hoping someone might come along and feel the need to give a stranger a ride, take me as far as they were going, then hoping someone else would do the same, and eventually find my way home.

A logging truck eventually pulled onto the shoulder as I stood there, its air brakes hissing, dust rising into the air, the driver motioning me to climb in. I climbed up and in.

"Where are you going, boy?" He asked.

"Cloquet, home." I replied. "Thanks for the ride."

"I'm going as far as Grand Rapids to dump this load. That'll get you halfway anyway."

"Where you coming from, boy?" He asked.

"Bemidji. I was up visiting relatives." I lied.

We didn't say much else to each other the next sixty or so miles. He had the radio on listening to a county music station. I'd never ridden in a big truck like that before, so high off the ground. The suspension was rough so we bounced along, its diesel motor rumbling. In just over an hour, we arrived in Grand Rapids, and he pulled off into a side street leading to a paper mill.

"This is where you get out, boy." He said to me, coming to a stop.

"Thank you, mister. Thank you for the ride." I replied. I climbed out and down and waved as he drove away.

I walked through the rest of the town, to a junction, one road going northeast toward the Iron Range cities of Hibbing and Virginia, the other to Duluth, eighty miles away. Home was thirty-five miles south of Duluth. Standing there on the side of the road, my thumb out with each passing car. I must have stood there a half an hour.

I saw the maroon color of a Minnesota Highway Patrol car coming toward me, too late for me to turn the other way so he couldn't see my face, too late to look for a place to run, hide. The car pulled over and stopped where I was standing, the officer turning on the car's flashing red lights. He sat in the car for a few moments, then opened the door, put on his Mountie hat, as they call it, and came around the side of the road to where I was standing.

"What you doing out here, young man? What's your name?"

"Simon. Simon Pendagayosh. I'm just walking home."

"How old are you, Simon? You know that hitchhiking is an unlawful offense, don't you?"

"I'm thirteen. No, sir, I wasn't hitchhiking. I am just walking home."

He looked me up and down. I, standing there, rumpled and tired from walking the entire night before, having less than an hour, at most, night of sleep on the bus north to Bemidji. He opened the rear passenger side door of the patrol car.

"Would you step inside the car for a few minutes, young man?"

I complied, never having been spoken to by a police officer before, let alone having sat in the back of a patrol car. We sat there along the side of the road for a long time while he called in to dispatch.

"Where are you from? What is your date of birth?" He asked, looking back at me. I complied.

I knew it was over then. Finally, after talking back and forth to dispatch, he turned to me. He got out of the patrol car and came around to the passenger side and opened the rear door.

"Step outside and turn around, young man. Put your hands on the car."

I was handcuffed, and he took me by the arm and put me back into the car.

From there, I was taken to the Itasca County Jail and turned over to the sheriff's office. I spent two days there in lockup, and was then transported to the Yellow Medicine County Jail in Granite Falls. I didn't ask what the charges I was being held for, and no one told me.

I spent another three days there in lockup and then was escorted by a sheriff's deputy, in handcuffs, to the courthouse. There, at just thirteen years of age, I was charged as a delinquent for the aggravated assault of Father Adrian.

"You are extremely fortunate he lived," the public defender said to me. "You could have easily killed him."

I admitted what I had done and told him why. I know he didn't believe a word of what I said about what the priest had done to Carolina, that no one would believe a priest would do that to a young girl.

Even now as an old man, I remember that day, standing before a juvenile court judge, as he sentenced me to three years at the juvenile reformatory in Red Wing, Minnesota. There, where I would spend the full three years. There, not a visit from my father or mother. I, realizing they were too poor to afford the long drive down from the reservation. Their old car would have never even made the trip. A letter, opened and screened by a Red Wing employee, arriving once a month from my mother, keeping me apprised of family matters.

Three years lost, parents, siblings.

And Carolina.

Part Two

CHAPTER EIGHT

My Life

Carolina

I spent weeks in an attempt to be assured Simon had made it home successfully, the first letter to him in secret so my parents might not know of him as I was considered too young to have a relationship with a boy. Sneaking into my parent's bedroom when they were not in the house to the top drawer of an old secretary desk, retrieving an envelope and stamp. Missing Simon terribly, not knowing a complete mailing address, simply putting his name, followed by Fond du Lac Reservation, Cloquet, Minnesota. It was returned, stamped insufficient address.

My mother, of course, found out straightaway as she collected the mail every day, that first letter to him returned back to me. She was waiting for me in the kitchen the day it came back. I remember we had a mother-daughter talk that day. Years later, I would remember that talk, and the others that would follow, and do the same with my daughters.

"Sit down, my girl," she said, pushing a chair out with her foot.

I, eyes cast downward to the floor, complied.

"Who is this boy, Simon?" she asked.

And I, lower lip quivering, trying my best to maintain composure. Knowing I would not be able to make something up, that the truth, or partial truth, was necessary.

"He helped me make it home."

"And did he leave the school when you did?"

I, crying softly by then, tears falling down on my dress, replied.

"Yes, he was leaving for his home too."

"I'm just trying to make sure he made it home alright," I said. "He is a friend."

None of what I told her was a lie. I just didn't tell the whole story, simply a part of it.

"Is this Simon more than a friend?" She asked.

Sobbing now, nose running, I wiped my face with my arm. A pause, I, speaking in the language of silence. And then, finally, whispering.

"Yes."

"Carolina," she said. "Come here, my girl."

I remember then, my mother holding me for the longest time, letting me cry softly until there were no more tears. And when I was finally done, she spoke to me again.

"Your father will never know of this, you understand."

"Yes, I understand."

From that day forward we shared that secret. And when I wrote other letters in my attempts to find out if Simon was safely home, unsuccessfully trying other addresses, a post office box, rural route, I would find them returned undeliverable, neatly tucked under my pillow, a secret held between my mother and I.

Finally, after weeks, I wrote no more letters. Acknowledging I would never be able to know if Simon was able to make it back home. I settled back into home, got enrolled at the public school in Bemidji, rode the bus back and forth to school each day with my sister and other kids from the reservation.

I would, on occasion, have terrible dreams of what had happened to me at the sister school. What the priest had done to me. Always, my sister would run into our parent's room and fetch our mother to wake me up.

"You were having one of them nightmares again," June would say the next morning. Sometimes she would tease me about them. To this day, I have never understood my sister well. We are now a couple of old women. Still, every once in a while, something meant to be a cutting remark will slip out of her mouth, some comment about this or that, targeting someone else, or me.

Always, my mother would awaken me whenever I had one of those dreams.

"Wake up, my girl," she would say, shaking me softly.

And I would awaken, eyes wide open, staring up at her.

Now an old woman, I remember when my mother became old and infirm, when she moved into our home with my husband Bill and me, and our little daughters, so I could care for her. How, every once in a while, I would awaken late in the evenings to the sound of her moaning and struggling, trying to free herself from whatever demons she was battling. I, the daughter, waking my mother.

I cannot say that my high school years in the public school were anything to write home about. It's not that I didn't do well in school, I did, taking the courses that were expected of women during that period, home economics, typing, bookkeeping, shorthand. I joined no clubs or extracurriculars. There were no girl's sporting teams at that time, it being long before Title IX. Most of us from the reservation lived too far from school to stay after the buses left. There was no late bus headed in the direction of our homes. Our fathers held jobs, if they were lucky enough to find work, that required long hours and low pay. There was no one who could pick us up after school for choir, band, speech club, drama, cheerleading, future homemakers.

Moreover, it was not like we would find ourselves welcomed there anyway. Racism, both covert, the subtle, hidden kind, and the overt racism, name calling and occasional violence against Native students, was ever present. In town, the police targeted Native people for arrest. Store clerks followed Native shoppers around their stores, expecting us to steal something. Some things never change. In many ways, our world is still that way.

Few, if any, of my fellow Native students, were in such extracurricular activities except the few who lived in town. The ones that fared better were the children of the Native people who worked in the Indian bureaucracy. The agency offices of the Bureau of Indian Affairs and Indian Public Health Service were all headquartered in Bemidji. These were the only good jobs available to Native people at the time, the men who worked there enjoying decent wages, living above the poverty level, having a nice car and home, able to buy new clothes for their children at the beginning of the school year. The Native women who worked for these agencies occupied the lower positions as secretaries, bookkeepers, assistants to this or that. The courses I took at Bemidji High School were preparing me for that.

Nevertheless, I got good grades. Memories of Simon faded. The night terrors I experienced lessened in frequency. I moved on with life, had Native boyfriends who I could meet up with at summer powwows, the infrequent teen dances sponsored by the reservation, or the Indian softball and basketball games and tournaments. We Native people back then had our own separate social gatherings. Native girls dated Native boys. The whites had their own social gatherings. White boys dated white girls. That was simply the way things were.

I cannot say I had a serious relationship with any of my teen boyfriends. None of them got beyond second base, as we called it back then, with me. I did my share of necking, even came home with a hickey once when I was seventeen that I had to hide with makeup. Like most teens, I experimented with drinking. More than once, a boy would try to get me drunk in hopes of taking advantage of me, but I knew when to quit. And I had girlfriends, all Native as can be like me. Girls who I could share secrets with, talk boys and life.

I graduated from Bemidji High School in 1961. I was on the B or A honor roll during most of my high school years. Our high school counselor met with all seniors that final year, and on the day he called me into his office to talk about possible careers, he told me I was well prepared to enter the workforce as a secretary or book-keeper if I didn't choose to become a housewife. Looking back now, I suppose I should have resented what he said, that he held such low expectations for young women at that time, Native girls in particular. During that time, however, that was what was expected of young women, of Native women.

I spent the summer following graduation powwowing, winning prize contests in Bois Forte and Grand Portage, living at home with my parents, tucking away my winnings. I applied for secretarial and bookkeeper jobs at the Bureau of Indian Affairs (BIA) and Indian Public Health Service (PHS), and come late July, got an interview for a bookkeeper opening at the BIA.

I did well in the interview and got a job as a bookkeeper in the agency office of the BIA in Bemidji. My parents helped me find a room to board in Bemidji. I started at low pay but worked my way up on the federal pay schedule. Federal jobs like that had decent pay and benefits. They still do.

There I worked for four years in the back offices, in accounts payable. It was decent work. I made friends, dated some of the young Native men who worked there, who held the higher, better paying positions because they were men. Summer weekends were consumed with powwowing. My vacation time was used for attending ceremonies. Many weekends were spent with my mother out in the bush, gathering medicines.

Our ways, what I did back then, ceremonies and gathering medicines, I kept separate from the people in my workplace. I've never been embarrassed for who I am or how I live. It's just that the people

I worked with, most all of them to be truthful, were on life and career paths that had little to do with their Native ways. Never once did I come upon any of them at summer powwows, ceremonies. I never recalled any of them talking about our ways, medicines, or using the language. I never spoke our language at work, only at home, or powwows and ceremonies. For all I know, few in my workplace could speak a word of the language, or cared to learn it. There was, and still is unfortunately, a whole segment of our Native people who have moved on from their Native ways, see little in it relevant or important in their lives. They may work in Native agencies, administering Native programs, or enforcing rules and regulations with regards to Native people. Their ways have become the American way, to make good money, buy a new car and live in a nice house, speak English only, yet be there in line whenever there is something free handed out on their rez. So, at my work there was this terrible dichotomy of working in an agency whose mission was to oversee the betterment of Native people, yet be peopled by individuals who were, at least to me, reluctantly Native. I hope that has changed.

My sister June, it turned out, became the same way. Upon graduating from high school, she moved to Duluth where she found a secretarial job at the state employment office, working for a man whose job it was to train and locate jobs for Native people. Once away from our parents and me we rarely heard word of her, except an occasional card at Christmas time. We never saw her at the powwows or ceremonies. Years passed and we pretty much lost touch with her. If I went to powwows at Fond du Lac, just thirty miles from Duluth, I'd try to contact her so I might visit, but she wouldn't return my letters, and later on my phone calls. The same would be true if I had to drive through Duluth on my way to Rendezvous Days in Grand Portage, the annual powwow celebration near the Canadian border. Letters and, later, phone calls, all gone unanswered.

Only many years later did I see her once when I made a quick stop in a downtown Duluth store where I was hunting for material to make a new outfit for one of my daughters, I came upon her walking down the street.

"June," I said, surprised. "How are you June?"

"Carolina," she said, looking toward me.

Neither of us quite knowing what to say to each other. Talking weather, the news. Our worlds grown far apart. She, now almost a stranger. We visited for only a few minutes, then awkwardly said our goodbyes.

"I'll see you later," I said.

"See you," she replied. Both of us knowing our chance meeting that day spoke loudly about how we had gone our separate ways.

My sister, reluctantly Ojibwe.

After four years working at the BIA, I decided maybe it was time to do something else with my life. The year was 1965. Scholarships had become available for Native students who wanted to attend vocational school or college. I knew I didn't want to move far from the familiar, and applied for a scholarship and sent in all the forms for acceptance at Bemidji State College, as it was called back then.

I was accepted, received enough of a mix of scholarships, grants, and a small student loan to pay my tuition and be able to live, and started college. I, one of the very few Native students to attend the college at the time. Our choices as women in the professions were somewhat limited then, teaching or social work. The memories of my days in elementary and high school not being the best, I chose social work. There I was for the next four years, studying casework, child custody, psychology, child welfare.

I did well enough in school. The last quarter there I did an internship for the Leech Lake Reservation, working at the Cass Lake Indian Hospital as a medical social worker. I was offered a job when I graduated, becoming one of the few Native professional social workers in the state of Minnesota, the only Native professional except for the director, working at the Indian hospital, where most Native people served mainly in maintenance, aide, and kitchen positions.

I worked at the Indian hospital until 1976, then took a position with the Indian Child Welfare Act (ICWA) Program at the Minnesota Chippewa Tribe (MCT) headquarters, just down the street from the hospital. There, my job was to license Native foster homes and oversee the placement of Native children into temporary and permanent foster care, as well work with Native families who wanted to adopt Native children. The job allowed for travel throughout the member reservations of the MCT, to state and national Native social work workshops and conventions.

I loved my work, of course, having the responsibility of ensuring that Native children were loved and protected. For too many generations, so many of our children had been placed into non-Native homes where their Native ways were ignored, forgotten, many times by well-meaning white foster parents. And other times they suffered abuse in all its forms in those homes. I have often wondered how what happened to me all those years ago at the sister school influenced the work I chose as an adult.

I worked in that position until I retired in 2008. The tribe had a big celebration for me. My daughters came to it. The tribal chair was there. She honored me with a Pendleton blanket, wrapping it around me up on the stage of the tribal center's gymnasium. The Leech Lake Singers did an honor song.

I've been blessed with a good life, surrounded, by and large, by good people, and a Creator, there up in that place beyond the stars, sending its blessings down upon me as I've walked *aki*.

⟶≫≫≫⟶

I met Bill, who would become my husband, at the Fourth of July Powwow in Red Lake when we were both in our early twenties. I, a champion fancy shawl dancer. He, a member of the Boyd family, one of the well-known men's fancy dancers from Inger, a small reservation community located about fifty miles north and east of Bemidji. Either he or his brother always seeming to be in competition for every championship at the powwows they attended, whether it be in Minnesota or the Dakotas.

At first, just small talk. Him teasing me. Me teasing him back, poking fun at each other. Telling Indian jokes. I remember whenever I really got a good one on him, he would laugh, saying,

"Aaaaaayyy . . ." That way we Native people can only say it. Then we would both laugh, me covering my mouth. He, hands on his hips, in his dance outfit, horse hair roach, black velvet beaded leggings and breach cloth, eagle feather bustle. Me in a dance dress I made of satin and ribbons, my hair back in beaded barrettes, wearing beaded moosehide moccasins my father had made for me.

Soon both of us out there in the powwow arena side by side during each inter-tribal dance, watching whenever we came back around the elder sitting area, our parents, now elderly, sitting there eating fry bread tacos, pointing at us with their lips.

"That's my girl out there." My mother

"That's my boy out there." Bill's mother.

The handsome couple, they said.

Our courtship lasted less than six months. We married the old time Ojibwe way.

When Bill made his intentions known to my father, he brought him a deer, cleaned, cut, packaged, and frozen, ready for the freezer, showing he would be a good provider to me, and later any children we might have. We each selected four elders to help us prepare for married life, give us advice, counsel. I chose one of my aunties as one of the four. On a morning several days before my wedding Auntie took me back in the bush to Lake Andrusia, where I bathed as a way to signify a blessing by *nimaama-aki*, mother earth. We feasted, visited, and held giveaways for three days. We gave gifts to all of those in attendance, any remaining food from the feasts to elders. The wedding was conducted by an elder pipe carrier under an arbor of cedar boughs. Then each of us took up a blue blanket and went into a fire circle, the fire of the different trees from the bush to represent the joining of our families into one. We tossed the blue blankets aside, and our mothers and aunties wrapped a white blanket around us, signifying the joining of our two lives together as one. Anyway, there are a lot of details about our ways. Too many, certainly than to try to explain them all.

I just know that Bill and I loved each other. And when my own daughters found everlasting love and married, they also followed their Ojibwe ways. I had made each of them a white dress and moccasins of elk hide for their weddings.

I bore and we raised two girls, twins, Andonis, my daughter, and Waawaatesi, Firefly. Both were raised strong in our Ojibwe ways. We spoke the language in our home, took them to ceremonies as babies and as long as they lived in our home. I taught them all that I know about the medicines we use in healing, the songs, prayers, and uses of the many plants.

We sent them to the tribal school where their Ojibwe ways were celebrated and honored. They grew and became strong Ojibwe women. One the director of a Native school in the heart of the Phillips neighborhood in Minneapolis. The other became a social worker like me, and is now teaching classes at Leech Lake Tribal College.

Bill and I continued our lives as dancers at every powwow we could attend. As we got older, I transitioned to become a jingle dress dancer, he a men's traditional dancer. He was there at my side, supporting me when my father passed. He willingly agreed to take my mother into our home when she could no longer care for herself. My girls helped care for her as well.

He worked for the BIA road crew, servicing the roads on the Leech Lake Reservation. Now as an old woman, I still see him sometimes in my dreams, coming through the door of our home after a day of work on the reservation covered with dust from operating a grader all day on the dusty roads that crisscross Leech Lake rez.

Bill got diabetes in his forties. Had to inject himself with insulin to try to control it. This went on for nearly twenty years. Eventually he couldn't work anymore. His heart was affected. We had to deal with infections. He lost a toe, then a foot, couldn't powwow dance anymore, so in summers I would push him from the car to a seat in the elder sitting area so he could watch. Watched as I was out there for grand entry in my jingle dress outfit, my eagle feather fan high in the air, dancing. Watched as I was out there when we honored our veterans. I danced for him, a veteran of the Vietnam War, where he had been injured by shrapnel. Where he had fought for a country that has never completely accepted its Native people as equal members of society, that continues to fight us for our treaty rights, for our desire to protect our animal relatives and *aki*, earth.

When he passed, I thought my world had ended. My daughters rushed home to be with me when it happened, took time off their jobs, took care of all the duties necessary to send him off in a good way. I, alone in our home in bed, grieving.

No one to wake me when I had those dreams. Those dreams of what happened there, at the sister school, all those years ago.

Nowadays I continue to do my volunteer work. I am an elder volunteer at a program designed to help our Native women who have been trafficked, have spent time out on the streets servicing men for a living, and for all the Native women who have been murdered by spouses, boyfriends, or killed while being trafficked. I spend time in a shelter for women who are just off the streets. My responsibilities aren't to try to convince them to quit their way of life. That is not our way to preach. I am there to be with them, lend an ear if they need one, pray for and with them if they ask.

They call me Auntie. I love each one of them, no matter who they are or their circumstances. No matter if they change their minds and go back to the streets, or come back again, I'm there for them. At night sometimes in the shelter when I'm there, and we gather in circle, I'll be there. Singing an old, old song I learned from my mother. One she learned in the lodge at ceremonies. Many of them young girls will begin crying then, releasing some of that hurt, that pain. Me, holding that *asemaa*, tobacco, in my hand, eyes closed tightly, facing up to where our Creator watches over us.

Singing.

And at other times I am there to pray with them, for them. This is one.

Nana'isanishinaam / Bring Us Peace

> *Gizhawenimimin Gichidibenjiged*
> > We are blessed by you Creator
> *ezhi-aanikoobidooyan gakina gegoo.*
> > you who connects all being.
> *Gizhawenimimin Giizis*
> > We are blessed by you Sun
> *ezhi-mashkawizi'iyaang.*
> > you give us light and strength.
> *Gizhawenimimin Dibiki-giizis*
> > We are blessed by you Moon
> *gikinoo'amawiyaang zaagaasidiyaang.*
> > you teach us the importance of reflection.
> *Gizhawenimimin Mashkiig*
> > We are blessed by you Land and Water
> *ezhi-ditibiziyan wenji-bimaadiziyaang.*
> > your circulation supports our living.
> *Apii zhawenimiyaang, zhawenimangidwaa.*
> > As we are blessed, we bless others.

Apii zaagi'iyaang, zaagi'angidwaa.
>As we are loved, we love others.
Apii noojimo'iyaang, noojimo'angidwaa.
>As we are healed, we heal others.
Apii inawenimigooyan, inawenindiyaang.
>As we are related to you, we are related to one
>another.
Naadamawishinaam daga noongom
>Help us all now
Nagamotawishinaam daga noongom
>Sing to us all now
Nanaa'ishinaam daga noongom
>Repair us all now
Nana'isanishinaam daga Gichidibenjiged.
>Bring peace to all our souls Creator.[5]

I also signed up as an elder volunteer at St. Luke's hospital. There, reading to children all colors, sizes, visiting the patients, listening, talking story, especially with the Native elders.

We all need to give back in some way.

This is my way. What I do.

CHAPTER NINE

My Life

My Father

> When thoughts become cluttered
> with anxiety, worry, this or that
> I find that quiet place in my mind
> and enter it
> there
>
> then in my imagining
> my father enters that space
> and sits beside me
> even knowing he walked on
> nearly sixty years ago
> when I was just a boy
>
> Sometimes he will talk story
> soft and low in the language
> but mostly he will simply nod to let me know

he is there
there in his red flannel shirt and cap
stained with sweat from cutting wood
and smelling of Old Spice and Prince Albert
he who spent the entirety of his life in the bush
I who traveled the world
he who ran away from the sister school at the age of twelve
and never looked back
I who was over-educated in the colonizer's schools
and came to use too many words
he who chose words sparingly, as if each was sacred
he who knew all the stories of the stars and the spirits who
                live there
could speak the why of all things
I who read books, memorized facts
defined my reality based on logic

all of that
the charade upon which I have defined my world
comes tumbling down
when he enters that quiet place
and reminds me

My father
there
sitting next to me

Simon

My father passed during my second year in Red Wing Reformatory.
I was fifteen years old. I remember I was in my room reading when

a knock came at the door. A worker, saying I was being called to the director's office.

"The director wants to see you," he said. "You'll need to come with me."

"Why?" I asked.

I had no idea why the director would want to see me. I hadn't been in any trouble that I knew of, or witness to any.

It was early spring, I recall. The weather was cold and cloudy. We left the dorm and crossed the yard, the ground still hard from winter, grass brown. When we arrived at the administrative building, I was made to sit in reception, the worker staying with me until I was called into the director's office. Finally, after what seemed like forever, the director's door opened and he motioned for me to enter.

"Come in, young man," he said, pointing at a chair. "Have a seat."

He went back behind his desk and moved some papers around, then picked up a pencil to fiddle with as he spoke.

"I'm afraid I have some bad news for you, son. Your father has died."

I caught my breath when he said those words. The room, him, the worker standing just outside the door, all suddenly surreal.

"My father?" I said, my voice shaking.

"Yes, I'm afraid so, son. The Carlton County Sheriff's Office called just a while ago to inform us. We'll be arranging travel for you," he continued. "To return home for the funeral, once we know when funeral arrangements have been made."

"Do you know how it happened?" I asked.

"We don't have any details. I'm sorry, son. I'm sorry I had to deliver this kind of news to you."

I have a vague recollection of the worker walking me back to my room, of me sitting there in silence and disbelief, later of being called to the dining hall, or being in classes for the next two days, sharing my grief with no one. Of lying in my cot at night, fitful dreams, trying to come to terms with the knowledge I would never see my father again, hear his voice.

Three days later, a worker drove me north on Highway 61 to Cloquet, west out of town to Reservation Road, then a few miles north to the little reservation church. We entered the parking lot and I could see the men of the community standing outside on the steps, talking and having smokes. Some distant cousins, gathered around the side of the church near the well pump, boys with their hands in their pockets, girls wiping their hair away and shielding their eyes from the sharp morning sunlight.

When we found a parking spot, the eyes of those outside shifted to us, there, sitting in a black State of Minnesota vehicle.

"Are you ready to go in, son?" The worker asked. I nodded back to him that I was.

I remember walking up the steps into the church, the men of the community parting for me to enter, some putting their hands on my shoulders to comfort me, one of my uncles stepping forward to take my hand and shake it.

"Simon," he said. Then I, my head down, hands neatly folded in front of me, stepping inside, moving slowly to the holy water, my hand dipping into it, then making the sign of the cross. Ahead of me, taking up the first four pews of the church, my family. Uncles and aunties and cousins sitting behind my brothers, sisters, and mother. My sisters and brothers, Annie, Johnny, Faith, Patty, Joshua, and Beau, sitting in one pew. Alexis, Terry, George, Mike, Robert, and Jim in another. There, just enough room for one more, next to Annie and Johnny, I genuflected and sat along side them. My older brother George, sitting in the front pew next to our mother, leaned over to whisper of my presence that I, Simon, the one in reform school, had arrived. Then she arose and came back to me and took me into her arms, crying softly. I, still sitting, arms by my side, trying my very best not to break down with her.

"My boy," is all she said to me. "My boy."

And soon enough, the church bells began tolling as the hearse carrying my father appeared over a small rise in the road coming toward the church, and the organ began to play. The church, filled with mourners, as well those who attended funerals regardless whether they knew or liked the deceased, now quiet. The priest and altar boys walking from the altar to the back of the church to meet my father's coffin. The pallbearers, all veterans, like my father. I looking back, his coffin draped in the American Flag. My father, a veteran of the war with Japan, a war he never spoke a word of once he returned home.

All of us now, his children, my mother, crying softly, my sister Annie holding my hand. I, trying to comfort her and my brother Johnny. My older brothers, trying their best to remain stoic, eyes straight ahead, red, an occasional tear rolling down their cheeks. One of my older sisters cradling our mother.

I remember when the mass ended, we all walked out to the cemetery, where the men of the community had prepared the gravesite. There, seven uniformed U.S. Marine veterans, greeting us, the priest saying the final prayers, one of the veterans playing taps, quiet sobbing of the women and girls, then three volleys from the veteran's rifles as tribute to our father's service to the country. The American Flag, then neatly folded and presented to our mother.

And all during this time, circling high above us, an eagle.

I got to stay until just after the luncheon provided by the women of the church, held in an old, sagging hall just across the road. I, sitting next to my mother, who told me my father had died walking home from work one day, just collapsed and died, she said, and his cousins hauled him up the hill when they realized he was already gone. Then the worker from the reformatory, who had sat in the car during the service and after funeral meal, finally coming into the hall and tapping me on the shoulder, informing me that it was time to leave.

I was to spend another year there in Red Wing, being released at the age of sixteen and given a bus ticket north to Cloquet. Riding home that day wearing state issued clothing and shoes.

Without our father's income my mother had to apply for county welfare for food, county clothing orders for school clothes, fuel orders for coal come winter. Too poor to afford presents, the VFW took one of us Christmas shopping, where we were limited to no more than two dollars each per present. My brothers and sisters helped when we could. In summers my brothers and I caught catfish from the river and sold it to neighbors, bringing some home to eat. In winter we snared rabbits to eat, and sold most. We worked for local farmers, picking potatoes, strawberries, throwing hay bales at harvest time. We went out in the bush and picked blueberries and sold them at the Sawyer Store. I got a job at the local summer carnivals, which came to town during the Fourth of July and Labor Day weekends, working the caramel apple and snow cone stand. All our earnings were given to our mother. We didn't give it a second thought.

Our family, however, without our father there, saw things break down. Slowly, at first. Some of my older brothers began stealing bikes from town kids and parting them out, selling them for smokes and beer they'd get from a runner, someone who would buy booze for underage kids for a pack of smokes or a few bucks. They burgled stores. Several sisters began running around, and then ran away from home, eventually ending up in foster care. I wasn't any better. I quit listening to my mother, doing what I pleased, going out to drink with friends on Fridays and not returning home until Sunday, hung over. Our mother, long suffering, trying to raise a large family on her own, washing clothes, hanging them out to dry, cooking starchy, fatty foods she received from welfare coupons and government commodities, dealing with both underage and adult children who were lost, out of control, drinking, raising hell.

The only thing, it seems, I did right was school. I was good at it. There in the Cloquet Schools I was able to excel, making the honor roll all grading periods. Returning for the eleventh and twelfth grades as the good Injun to the town boys.

"Where you been all these years, Simon?" I remember one of them asking when I returned there for the eleventh grade.

"I moved for a while," I lied.

Come my senior year I was thinking about attending university. Even though my homelife was often chaotic, I had remained free of any further run-ins with the law. I, waiting until my eighteenth birthday when I would be released from probation, when my juvenile record would be expunged. I remember going in to see the school counselor to talk college. I had already made plans to take my ACT's, the college entrance exam, catch a ride into Duluth on the greyhound bus, hike up to the University of Minnesota Duluth campus, the test site, then return home once I had completed the test.

I remember the day I visited the high school counselor, sitting leaned back in his chair when I entered his office.

"Simon," he said. "What can I do for you?"

"I'm wondering," I said, "If you could help me with college. My family doesn't have any financial support for me, but I know there are loans, and maybe some grants out there I could apply to."

He dug out my school file, sitting there, putting on his reading classes.

"I think," he said, "you might need to think more realistically."

"There are some good trade schools. Dunwoody in the Twin Cities, the vocational institute in Duluth. You could look into the welding program at either one, or auto mechanics, carpentry maybe. These are good vocations. The pay is good. You'd be able to get in the union."

I, having no interest in being either a welder or carpenter. I, who wanted to become a poet, write a book. I, the good Catholic boy, whose last time in church was to attend his father's funeral, and before that to bludgeon the priest at the sister school who raped Carolina, sat there saying nothing. Hands neatly folded in my lap, looking straightaway past him, out the window. Sitting there saying nothing, the Indian boy who was not good enough, smart enough, for university, who was only good with his hands.

I graduated from Cloquet High School in the year 1962 near the top of my class. The day before graduation I walked from the reservation to the county welfare office in Carlton, Minnesota and back, over seven miles each way, to pick up a clothing order so I would have decent clothes to wear on graduation night. On my way home, I stopped at the town's only clothing store and bought a new shirt and pants, and a sport's coat that was hanging on the bargain rack, took it all home where my mother ironed it. That evening, I, Simon Pendagayosh, graduated with honors.

Without help or advice of anyone, I filled out the financial aid application and admissions forms to attend the University of Minnesota campus in Minneapolis, intending to earn a degree in English, with a specialty in creative writing. I spent the summer before university working odd jobs, giving most to my mother to help make ends meet. I received a favorable acceptance letter from university admissions, as well another from the financial aid office awarding me enough in grants and a loan to be able to pay tuition, books, fees, and housing.

In the fall of 1962 at the age of eighteen, my mother, then looking so much older and more tired than her years, sister Annie and brother Johnny, walked me down the trail through the bush, past the wood mill to downtown Cloquet, to the bus station. Now an old man, I remember that day. My mother a woman of few words, like my father.

"*Ningozis*, my son," she said. The first from our family to go to university. The school boy, the good Injun, the good Catholic boy. My brother and sister standing there beside her, squinting in the late afternoon sun.

"*Ni-mamaa*, my mother," I said. Too reserved to tell my mother I loved her, to thank her for all of the sacrifices she made so I could be there, that day. Too much caught up in thinking of my own future to acknowledge all the suffering I had caused her, as well my father, and the things I had done to dishonor them, my family.

Then, the bus slowly pulling away. I, looking out the window, as my mother, brother ,and sister disappeared. I, thinking.

My life, my life.

For the most part, I did well in university, except for occasions when my drinking became an issue. Partying often began on Thursdays and lasted much of the weekends. All of my drinking friends were non-Native. I did my best to make up my school work when I was sober.

I had my share of the opposite sex, white girls who I met at the frequent parties I attended, who were intrigued by alcohol, about having a Native boyfriend. In my years there at university, however, I never had a serious relationship. My life revolved around school, partying. Memories of Carolina, my first and only love at the mission school, faded.

"You Indians sure can drink," my friends would say to me, their official Indian, the Indian friend, always prefaced by the adjective, representing all the Native people in the world, all tribes. I, however, reveling as well in my coursework, creative writing, beginning and intermediate non-fiction, screenwriting, poetry and writing poetry, fiction and advanced fiction, writer's workshop, narrative craft, short story, television writing, memoir and personal essay, novel, writing editing, playwriting, and writing for life.

In my senior year I signed up for a study in Europe program focusing on European writers. I flew on my first airplane, traveling first to New York City, then crossing the Atlantic to London, taking a train north to the University of Birmingham. We traveled throughout England and Scotland, France, Italy, Spain, spending a full semester studying the great European writers, including, among many others, Daniel Defoe, Voltaire, Rudyard Kipling, Chaucer, Alice Werner, Charles Dickens, Shakespeare, Cervantes, Victor Hugo, Robert Burns,

Jane Austin. The thought never crossed my mind that all during my years in university did we ever once focus on writers from minority or Native communities. That all the people who were considered as great novelists or poets were primarily of European or European-American descent. Only until I was older and out of university did I discover the beauty in the stories and poetry by America's Black, Latino, and Native writers.

I rarely returned home to family. I worked summers waiting tables and bartending near campus. For the most part, my life and theirs led down different roads. They remained on the reservation, made their lives there. Some never completed high school, ended up with jobs working for the tribe in maintenance, building security, or in town at one of the paper mills. The several who completed high school ended up in secretarial and bookkeeping positions with the tribe. One brother became a tribal politician, being elected to represent the Cloquet district on the tribal council.

I graduated in 1966 from the University of Minnesota with a degree in English. As far as I could tell, I was one of only a few Native graduates from the university that year. None of my family attended my graduation ceremonies. My mother had never traveled farther than the city of Duluth, some thirty miles from the reservation. My brothers and sisters, too busy living their own lives. I, having distanced myself from them as a result of getting an education, of moving far from reservation life.

Drinking was becoming more of an issue to me. By then, at the age of twenty-two, I was probably a full-blown alcoholic, functional, however, still able to separate my drinking from work. Able to make it to wait jobs on time, smile, serve tables, many times still with a buzz going, or hung over. The same true with bartending, where I had access to drinking while on the job, could maintain the façade of sobriety until after closing time and cleanup.

Sometimes at night after waiting tables or bartending I would return to my room and try to write. I never could, sitting there for hours trying to craft a word into more, a poem, story. And always I would end up with little worthy of keeping the next day. Nothing worth sharing, or sending off to poetry reviews.

That part of me, the would-be poet, slowly and surely eventually fading from me.

I was able to land a job at the Midtown Indian Center as editor of their newsletter, reporting program news, recipes, happenings in the Twin Cities Native community, as well handling internal and external flyers and press releases. No more waiting tables or standing behind the bar. I was familiar with the center, having gone there on occasion for community events, powwows, or speakers. Becoming over-educated did not mean I had forgotten to still be Native. My education may have allowed me to become able to mingle in non-Native social circles, to stand around and chitchat with bigwigs and other influential people, but I still remained comfortable among my own people. I, retaining the ability to speak our language, respected, I suppose, by many of the Native people who worked there who hadn't been exposed to the language when young, by parents who didn't want their children to learn the language. Parents who had been traumatized in the boarding and mission schools, who had been programmed to think that speaking English was the future, that our language represented the past. Others who had parents who had the language beaten out of them. Or, whose parents, if they could speak the language, did so only when their children weren't present, or only when around each other at gatherings, where they would sit in their circles, speaking it in whispers so their young couldn't hear. Speaking in whispers, like they had been forced to do in the boarding and mission schools they had attended, away from the nuns, priest, teachers, matrons. Like

Carolina and I had to do all those years ago behind the dorm at the sister school.

I worked at the Indian center for three years, my drinking slowly getting the better of me, until one day the director and human resources coordinator called me in and informed me that I was missing too much work, calling in late too often, or not calling in, not showing up at the job. That co-workers could smell the alcohol on my breath. That sometimes I would return from lunchtime slurring my words.

"We think you need to seek help," they said.

"But I don't have a problem," I replied, indignantly.

"We think you do," They replied. "We'd like to offer you some options. You can go to a counselor and be assessed for your chemical use. If you are in need of treatment, you will do that. We'll give you a leave of absence. When you successfully complete it, you can return to your job."

"And what if I refuse?" I asked.

"Then I am afraid we'll have to let you go."

"Then I quit," I said, standing up, and walking out.

We make decisions like this in the course of our lifetimes, ones without any forethought, out of emotion, without logic. We take the left path when the right one was the way to go. We decide this, instead of that. Now as an old man I sometimes think how my decision to walk out on my job there rather than seek counseling, treatment, would affect the rest of my life.

I had rent, bills to pay. I needed work. So, I put my application in for other professional positions within the Native community. I was, after all one of a handful of university educated Native professionals in the Cities, the state for that matter. Meantime, I found part time jobs waiting tables, tending bar. I moved into a rooming house, a room with a single bed and dresser, bathroom down the hall. I ate on the cheap, ramen noodles, meals from the restaurant where I worked, pickled eggs and nut goodies where I was part time bartender.

And I drank. Every other evening became every night. Never having enough money to have a decent living, but always enough to drink. My friends were other drunks I met at the Indian bars. Eventually able to land professional positions in several of the Twin Cities Indian programs because of my credentials, but never able to hold them for very long. Six months, nearly a year. I'd keep applying and sometimes get interviews. Several times I missed the interviews. Once I applied to a master's program in English, figuring I could land scholarships intended for Natives and minorities to live on. I was accepted into the program but never followed through with the scholarship applications. My life became a revolving door of dreams unfulfilled, of half starts, of promises I made to myself that I eventually broke. I'd stop the drinking so I could do this. Then maybe I'd cut down, enough so I could hold the job. This went on for several years, slowly spiraling into the abyss.

Meantime, I avoided family contact. I'd get letters from my mother and sister Annie, filling me in on family and community news. We missed you at this. We hope you can come up for that. Me, when I did write back, telling them I would try to get up there someday. And they would tell me there were now plenty of jobs with the tribe for people like me, that non-Natives filled most of the professional positions there when what they really wanted were tribal members to fill the spots. You'd get hired in a minute, they said.

I don't recall the moment that I first ended up on the streets. I'd been frequenting the Indian bars, drinking with others who were couch crashing, living off friends or enabling relatives because they couldn't afford to make do on their own. And there were some who relied on the feeding programs of churches and foundation funded programs for their meals, and an occasional place to sleep. Behind on rent, with no place to turn, I ended up in a rooming house with another drinker, sleeping on the floor until the manager found out. Then out on the street, then sleeping on the couch of another drinker. Then to a shelter when I was sober, or just coming down. Then to a feeding center, where I would stand in line for a meal. I made a little money busking on street corners playing my flute, just enough for an occasional bottle and some smokes.

This went on for years.

I, the smart one, the good Injun. The good Catholic boy.

It's not that I spent the next thirty years drinking. I had many periods of sobriety, days, months, several times nearly a year, where I sobered up, found enough work to rent a room, waiting tables, day labor. Sometimes my head clear enough to sit up late at night and write.

Always thinking of my mother and father, what they would think of me, what I had become. The shame, self-loathing keeping me from going home. My mother, drawn and worn down from life, trying to create normalcy after my father died. Still, whenever I had an address long enough for her to contact me by letter, she would always begin with

"My boy."

All the love she had for me contained in those two words. Even now, an old man, I still remember the sound of her voice.

My father, who worked hard so his family never went cold or hungry, who taught his sons the art and skills of lacrosse, who would take me out far in the bush with the dogs come winter, me riding in the sled with him on the back runners, the only sounds the panting of the dogs as they made our way down the trail, the runners in the snow. Him, talking softly on occasion to me, the dogs, always in the language.

My Life

My father, whose memory would sometimes come and visit me in late evenings in wherever I found myself, a rooming house, someone's couch, shelter, in a tent under a highway overpass.

My father
there
sitting next to me.

CHAPTER TEN

Coming Home

Simon

The world can be a pretty rugged place. We Natives sometimes use the English word, rugged, to describe some of life's more difficult times. I remember hearing once that for Native people things will only get better for us when we hit bottom. Someone else said that maybe for us there is no bottom. I hope that's not the case.

Losing loved ones, my father and mother, siblings Patty, Johnny, and George, they were rugged times. Being drunk at my mother's funeral must have been awful, humiliating for the rest of my family. I'd never even made it to my sister or brothers' funerals, have always wondered what the rest of my family thought of my absence. He's drunk, I'm sure they thought, and they were right. The simple act of not showing up was pretty rugged. And many years ago, at the sister school when the priest did that terrible thing to Carolina, that was really rugged. What I did to the priest afterwards was rugged.

You get my point.

I'd been dry this time for over five months, hanging by the skin of my teeth like I'd done too many times to count. Working day labor. Sober I was dependable, always showed up on the job on time, working hard, got along with everyone. Spent my lunch time reading novels by some of the Native authors I'd heard or read about—N. Scott Momaday, Sherman Alexie, Vine Deloria, Gerald Vizenor, Louise Erdrich, and others. I'd read Momaday's book, *The Way to Rainy Mountain*, over fifty times. His writing was, at least to me, the work of a literary genius. In evenings I'd read poetry. Again, my favorite was Momaday, this time from the book, *The Gourd Dancer*, to be more specific, the poem "Plainview: 2," where he told the story about an old man who grieved the loss of his horse. What I found fascinating about this poem in particular was the way in which it was crafted, to the cadence of a horse running, of hooves.

> I saw an old Indian at Saddle Mountain
> who drank and dreamed of drinking
> And a blue-black horse.[6]

I'd never been just some dumb reservation Indian, as some non-Natives liked to refer to us. I'm one of those over-educated, well-read, articulate ones, at least when I'm sober. I'd always cleaned up pretty good.

The world was changing, I just wasn't sure it was for the better. The streets had become more rugged, more crime, homelessness. I, sixty-one years old, having spent over half of that time *giiwashkwebii*, a drunk. I imagine my liver was kicking and screaming by then as well, and if it could talk it would be telling me to knock it off. Sometimes I'd still frequent the streets when I was sober, just to get out of my room, walk around, sit in a park, take a city bus nowhere special, ride the metro to downtown, window shop.

In the mid-1970s when I'd first ended up on the streets, the homeless were mainly men. Men of all colors and sizes. Few old men, of course, the streets claimed many early. As the years passed, especially along Franklin Ave, there were more Native men, and sometimes women, coming in from the reservations, as far as Pine Ridge, Rosebud, Sisseton, and, of course, all the northern Ojibwe reservations. I imagine they came into the city like I had, to get schooling, training or a job. Then things fell apart, like what happened with me. Maybe their woman and kids left them and headed back to the rez and their little world crumbled, turned to crap, and they ended up on the streets. Maybe the family back on the rez got tired of them slumming off them, always wanting money for booze or smokes, so they gave them the boot. There are a thousand different stories, all rugged.

On one of my walks, I'd come upon a Native family living under an underpass. Rare to see a family out living on the streets back then. I first saw their tent and knew right from the get-go whoever occupied it was Native because there was a pole next to it with ribbons in the colors of the four sacred directions and feathers tied to its top.

Sometimes when I was sober like that I'd stop and visit people. I remember mentioning that being sober can sometimes mean being lonely. If I had a few extra bucks on me, I'd bring along a pack or two of smokes along to give away, or some bread and peanut butter. I knew what hunger was like. That day I stopped by the tent, pretended to knock on the flap.

"Hey *neej*, friend, anyone in there?" I asked.

A Native woman unzipped the flap. I could see two small children inside, kneeling beside her, eating cookies or crackers or something.

"Sorry," I said. "I just wanted to see if you all are okay, or maybe need something."

I remember she looked back at me, suspiciously.

"What do you want?" she asked. One never knows what to expect when someone comes calling to your tent. They could be there to steal, rob, harass, even cause harm.

"Me? I don't want anything. I just wondered if you need anything."

"No," she said, and closed the flap.

A few days later while out for my walk I picked up a bag of ready to eat food and supplies, toilet paper, paper plates and plastic dinnerware from the Dollar Tree and set it outside the tent flap. Early the next evening on my way by the underpass I noticed the bag was gone. So, a few days later I did the same, leaving a bag of food items just outside the tent.

Late March can still be bone-chilling cold in Minnesota, and it can snow well into May. I always watched the evening news, read the newspaper, so I knew anything was possible as far as the weather was concerned. I noticed on WCCO television one night the weather person was calling for a dip in temperatures over the upcoming weekend. I was hoping the woman and her children would have gone to one of the shelters, accepted some help.

That Sunday morning, I walked down to the corner and bought a newspaper, hoping to spend the day reading, maybe try to write something of my own. When I got back to my room I opened the paper, and there in the local news was a short spread about the police finding a homeless woman and two children asphyxiated, apparently from using a small propane heater inside their tent. The article stated she had moved to Minneapolis recently from Kenora, Ontario. The person who found them said they had moved to escape an abusive domestic relationship, make a better life. I dropped the newspaper on the floor, put on my coat, and walked the half mile down to the underpass where the family had been living.

I could hear the singing from a block away, voices, a hand drum. When I got to where the tent had been, there were several Native people standing on the sidewalk, a woman with a hand drum, accompanied by another woman, singing a mourning song. Someone had put a bouquet of flowers on the ground near where the woman and her children had died. It was on Sunday, March 21, 2005.

The song.

Gimikwenimigo (We Remember You)

    Gimikwenimigo giizis ezhi-zaagiiaasigeyan
        We remember you sun how you shine
    Gimikwenimigo dibiki-giizis baabaabii'oyan
        We remember you moon waiting
    Mikwendaagozidaa apane gosha
        We should all remember always
    Mikwendaagozidaa apane gosha
        We should all remember always
    Gimikwenimigom aanikoobijiganag
        We remember the connected ancestors
    Gimikwenimigom inawemaaganag
        We remember all our relatives
    Mikwendaagozidaa apane gosha
        We should all remember always
    Mikwendaagozidaa apane gosha
        We should all remember always[7]

That was the day I made the decision never to drink again.

It took time before people started to believe I was actually going to stay sober. When you are a chronic alcoholic, everyone expects a relapse. I just know that it was returning to my Ojibwe ways that helped me maintain my sobriety.

I saw a poster at one of the Indian centers for a men's healing sweat, that Native men were welcome. So, I signed up, and took the bus to where it was conducted one evening, behind a home on the Southside. Here I was, sixty-one years old and I'd never been to a sweat before. I'd never participated in ceremony. As a baby I was baptized Catholic but hadn't been in a church since my mother's funeral years ago. I'd lost faith in it after what happened to Carolina at the sister school. As far as I was concerned, I viewed the church and it's teaching as hypocritical. Yet, upon occasion during my years on the street, I'd been subjected to religious indoctrination from the prayers and services conducted by Christian charities who offered food and, or shelter for street people.

The person conducting the sweat was an Ojibwe man, much younger than me. He introduced himself to me in the language, and realizing he was a speaker, I returned his greeting. His name, Deacon, from Lac du Flambeau. The other young men that came for the sweat that evening did not possess any degree of language fluency beyond *miigwich*, thank you, and *aniin*, hello. Yet, even though each of them was much younger than me and did not speak the language, I could tell they were much more knowledgeable than me in the protocol of the sweat lodge. So, I did what has always worked when I didn't know what to do. I practiced silence and observation.

I know now the way sweats are conducted are different, depending on who leads it. The young man conducting the sweat handed each of us *asemaa*, tobacco, when we approached him. He told us to offer it to the fire that had been built in his back yard, which was being tended by a firekeeper, a Native boy who was being trained in traditional knowledge so he one day could lead the sweat.

The fire heated the grandfathers, rocks, until they glowed. The fire and door of the lodge faced the east. I know now that, depending on the teacher, the sweat may face any of the other three directions. The lodge itself was framed in willow. I know now it can be framed in other woods as well, jack pine, maple, birch, ash. The lodge was round, domed, covered with tarps.

We sat in a circle once we entered the lodge, and the conductor closed the flap. There in perfect darkness, until he summoned the firekeeper to bring in the first set of seven grandfathers, cradled in deer antlers. The grandfathers were set in a pit in the center. Cedar water was poured on the red-hot stones, and the lodge became very hot. That first sweat, I had trouble breathing. In time, seven more grandfathers were added.

The young man conducting the sweat prayed in our language, then translated the best he could into English. He used a hand drum as he sang and conducted prayers. Then he began passing the drum around to each of us. The young men in the lodge with me each told why they had come to the sweat that evening, each with their own troubles. Eventually, the drum made it my way.

I remember I was quiet for a long time, not knowing quite what to say. I'd never shared part of myself before in that way, never opened my heart to strangers. Yet there was something about the ceremony that evening that worked its magic on me. Those healing spirits telling me that I was safe there, that telling my story, or part of it, would keep me on a healing path. So, I started to speak in our language, telling them about my years on and off the streets, of my struggles with alcohol, and about finally making a decision to become sober. All in the language. When I was done, I was ready to hand the drum over to the next person, but the young man conducting the sweat began to speak, praying at first in the language, then speaking to the young men around me in English.

"We are so honored to have our elder here this evening, to have him share a part of his story with us, to speak to us about his struggles, to show us in his words there is a way out of all of that pain we carry."

Then in the language he asked me if it was alright if he could share the story I had told, and I nodded that it would be.

Deacon shared, in English, what I had told them. And after the sweat was over and we left the lodge for a feast in the conductor's home, the young men came to me one by one and thanked me for my words. And before I left later that evening, the young man conducting the ceremony invited me to come again, as many times as I wanted.

Now, years later, I still stay in contact with him on my Obama phone. We rez Indians sometimes call the free phones we get from the tribal council "Obama" phones, because the free one-thousand-minute phone program began during the Obama administration.

That young man, Deacon, who conducted the sweat is not so young anymore.

"Uncle," the not as young anymore sweat lodge conductor will say to me when he picks up the phone whenever I call him. The highest praise you can offer an elder teacher.

There were other things I became involved in once I quit drinking. At one of the Indian centers, I noticed on the bulletin board a men's group that met once a week, so I made my way to it one evening. There were a small group of us that evening, sitting in a circle, some Dakota, Ho-Chunk, and Ojibwe men. They served strong, black coffee and one of them had brought a dozen day-old sweet rolls to share. The man who led the group was Dakota from Sisseton. He prayed in his language to begin, then we went around and introduced ourselves. When it was my turn, I introduced myself in English and my language. When I said where I was from, *Nagachiwanong*, Fond du Lac Reservation, one of the men on the other side of the circle said he too was from there. He asked me if I was related to any of the other Pendagayosh's who lived there, rattling off names of several of my sisters and brothers, and other names I didn't recognize, possibly nieces, nephews who I had never met.

"Do you make it back home very often?" He asked.

"*Gaween*, no," I responded. "I've been on a pretty rugged road for quite a while now. I'm just starting to think clearly. No, I haven't been home in years. I guess I've lost touch."

"Me too," he said. "I was born here in the Cities, but am enrolled up there. I might know names of some people, but it's only what I get second-hand from talking to my parents."

The discussion that night really wasn't like a recovery gathering. We talked about different things, cultural teachings, language loss, problems in our communities. Some of the men spoke about issues they were dealing with, or had dealt with, their own drinking, drugging, being unemployed or underemployed, run-ins they'd had with the law. I, listening. Maybe I just wasn't ready to share much. I went back, however, the next week and the next, and slowly, opened up more, sharing a bit more of my story.

Several members of the men's group were drum members and eventually asked if I was interested in joining them. I suppose they thought I had that background because of my language ability. Little did they know I had never sat at a drum before, didn't know a thing about the songs or protocol. I had played the flute, of course, for years, songs I'd made up. The flute was one of the ways I had made drinking money when I was out on the streets. I was a busker, laying down a blanket on a busy downtown street corner and playing my flute. People would come along. Some would stop and listen. Others would give me their pocket change. Those with money to burn would leave me a few bucks. When I had enough for a bottle, or some smokes, I'd close up shop and head to a liquor store. None, if any of them ever knew that the songs I played on that flute, I just sort of made up along the way. I just made sure it sounded authentically Native.

My other music of choice had pretty much been classic country, Vince Gill, Alison Krauss, George Jones, Waylon, Willie, Loretta Lynn. Bar music.

I laughed when the men of the drum group asked me to join, saying I didn't know anything. They said come anyway.

They drummed at one of their homes just off Cedar Ave so I went there the evening they told me to show up. I took the bus down. We visited for a while, then we all sat down around the drum. One of them handed me a drum stick. I just listened that night. The next week I tried my hand with the drum stick. Within a month I was mouthing some of the songs and after several months I was singing along, quietly at first, then as my confidence grew, I was singing along to the songs. Slowly finding my way back to culture. The men's group, drumming. I may have been brought up with the language, but I really didn't know much in a cultural sense, so all of it was a new, wonderful awakening for me. I was with that group of singers for years. We sang at a lot of gatherings in the Twin Cities.

Somewhere along the way on my path to sobriety I found purpose. We humans all need that to give our lives meaning. Now an old man, I realize the time we are here on *aki*, earth, is short, that we need to ensure we make good use of our time here. And I don't mean by that we need to find a job we like, or make money. I mean we need to make a mark, leave some kind of legacy, do something for others, be worthwhile. So, I began, on a regular basis, bringing bags of ready to eat food and smokes to the street people up and down Franklin Avenue, many of whom I knew. They would often offer me a drink, and I would respectfully decline. I remember doing the same, sharing smokes or what I had to drink, when I was living on the streets, characteristic of street culture. Other times, I'd just leave the bags outside their tent, or on top of the grocery carts of those who pushed all their worldly possessions around with them. I volunteered at one of feeding centers one evening a week, serving food. It was important for me to keep busy, and at the same time, give back.

During the weekdays I was working my job at day labor. In evenings it was men's group, drumming, volunteering at the feeding center, reading, writing. Weekends I spent shopping at Dollar Tree for cheap food goods and distributing, as much as I could afford, to the people living on the streets. In evenings I would read and do some writing. As time went on, my thoughts became more and more clear, and the words began to flow from my head onto paper.

One night before the men's gathering, I noticed a posting on the bulletin board for an Ojibwe language teaching position at Phillips Neighborhood Academy, a charter school catering to young people living in the Phillips neighborhood and Little Earth Housing. Ever since the mother and her two young children had been found dead in their tents nearly a year before I had wondered what I could do to work with young people. The job listing indicated a preference for a teaching degree or the eminence credential licensure as an Ojibwe language teacher, proficiency validated by a group of language speakers. I hadn't held a professional position in over thirty years, didn't have a resume, copies of my university transcripts, or driver's license, just a state identification card. One thing in my favor was that I didn't have a police record which would have automatically eliminated me from working with children once they did a background check.

That night I went home and worked up my resume. There was, of course, a large gap in professional employment that would stick out like a boil when it was reviewed, but I figured if I didn't apply it would be worse than not applying at all. After work the next day I rushed to the Indian center and met with a job developer and asked if she could have it typed and printed. I also asked her if she could go online and order me a copy of my university transcript, which she did.

I didn't have a contact phone number or email for the school to contact me should they be interested in giving me an interview, so the job developer offered to allow me to use her work phone number.

"Just check in every other day or so," she said. "In case they call and want you to come in for an interview."

So, I went to the Indian center every other weekday for several weeks. No calls. Then one day, a phone message telling me to call to set up an interview day and time. I used the job developer's phone.

On the day of my interview, I took time off my day labor job. The job developer, bless her heart, loaned me twenty dollars from her own pocket so I could go to the Salvation Army store to buy a decent pair of pants, shirt, and shoes. I scrubbed up good, slicked my hair back with some men's VO5, and took the bus down to the school.

The director there was a pleasant young Ojibwe woman, Andonis Boyd. She, as it turned out, was the screening and hiring committee. The entire interview was done in our language. Two of the inquiries.

"So, Uncle, tell me about the last thirty years. I see you've had day labor jobs."

"I was on a thirty-year drunk," I replied, truthfully.

"And how long have you been sober?"

"Nearly a year now."

At the end of the interview, she gave me a tour of the classrooms, each filled with beautiful brown, black, white, and mixed children. When we returned to her office she offered me the job, teaching kindergarten through six grade Ojibwe language. When I heard those words, my eyes welled up. I couldn't help it. She noticed, and her eyes welled up as well.

"Simon Pendagayosh," she said, wiping away her tears and smiling. "Look at what you made me do."

I taught there for the next nine years, until I was seventy-one years old, 2015, when I retired. Each school day, entering the classroom, beautiful, beautiful children of all colors, coming up to me, hugging me.

"Good morning, Uncle," each would say.

"*Niniijaanis*, my child," I would reply.

I could write a whole book about my years there.

<hr>

Still, during the years after I had quit the alcohol, gotten off the streets, been teaching and volunteering, I had never once returned to *Nagachiwanong*. I don't know why. Too many years gone, too many bridges crossed. My sister Annie, the only contact I had with my family, continued to call and write to me and make an occasional trek on the Greyhound bus to visit. By then I had my own small apartment just off Cedar Avenue. When she visited, I would take her to the feeding center where I volunteered an evening a week, and during the day to my classroom, where she got to meet my students.

I remember it was a January evening when she called. She was crying, telling me her husband had just passed, a massive stroke. Over the years, of course, she would ask me to return home. And always I had promised I would, one day.

The evening she lost her husband she asked me again.

"Brother," she said. "Brother, come home. Please."

I, realizing she needed support then. That her need for support was more than my reticence to return north. As soon as I hung up the phone, I stuffed a change of clothes into my knapsack, some toiletries, flute, and writing. Late in the afternoon the next day I took a city bus to the Greyhound bus depot downtown and bought a ticket north up I-35 to Cloquet.

I hadn't been home in years and the last time I was there I had been drunk at my mother's funeral. I, the drunk brother, the long lost, once many, many years ago the good Injun, the smart one, the good Catholic boy.

Going home.

I remember it was dark and bitterly cold when we arrived at the bus stop in Cloquet, a convenience store, gas station located at the junction of Highway 33 and Big Lake Road, just several miles from the reservation. There was some wind, fresh snow swirling, temperature in the teens below zero. Annie's home a mile or more away near Scanlon, a neighborhood on the east side of town. Me, not really prepared for such weather, although I was wearing warm socks, hiking shoes, gloves, coat, cap, and neck scarf, nothing warm enough for that kind of weather.

Walking to my sister's home, second guessing myself whether I should have made the trip in the first place, maybe consoled her on the phone instead, sent flowers, a card. Tired, I had slept little the night before, hadn't eaten or drunk much in the way of liquids, coffee or water.

About halfway there, taking side streets, few if any cars going by. Then suddenly feeling light-headed, faint, I stopped, hoping it would pass.

Then, just blackness.

CHAPTER ELEVEN

A Song Remembered

Carolina

When my husband Bill died, it seemed all promise died with him. We had been married for nearly thirty years, in many ways like one person. We went everywhere together, were rarely apart. Those infrequent times my work took me out of town I would always call him in the evenings, just to talk. Back in the days of long-distance landline telephones, we'd ring up quite a phone bill.

My daughters arranged for the traditional funeral to be held at our house in Pennington, out in the bush on the north side of Cass Lake. One of our relatives built the mourning fire out in our yard, which he, other relatives, and men from the lodge tended for four days, as is our tradition. People came from all over, Red Lake village, Ponemah, Inger, Deer River, Onigum, Naytahwaush, Ball Club. There to pay their respects, put *asemaa*, tobacco in the fire, pray, bring sweets or a casserole into the house and offer their condolences to my daughters and me. Many stayed for hours, long into the evenings, sitting and visiting, talking and laughing softly, respectfully, returning the next day, and the next. Smokers would go in and out of the house whenever they needed to light up, stand by the mourning fire, laughing and teasing one another. We Ojibwe even tease during difficult times.

All during the four days of the wake, the casket was in our living room, facing west, again, as is custom. Bill's brother, Damien, conducted the traditional service, leading us through the prayers and songs for the dead. For the burial, his body was wrapped in birchbark, his feet pointing west toward the land of souls. Some of his personal effects were placed with him for his journey, a medicine pouch, which I ensured contained everything he would need, hunting knife, deer rifle. He wore a new pair of moosehide moccasins, lovingly beaded by one of the nieces.

My period of mourning was a year. During that time, I did not participate in powwows. I wore drab clothing. Every year on the anniversary of his passing my daughters and I hold a feast to commemorate his life. All relatives, lodge members, and people who knew and worked with him are invited. A separate setting is placed at the dining room table for him. These are our ways. As the years have passed, of course, the number of people who show up for the feast has dwindled as those who knew him age or pass themselves. And unfortunately, many of our young people have never learned enough of our ways to continue the tradition. These annual feasts to honor those who pass will probably soon fade and disappear.

My sister June actually showed at the funeral. My girls, Andonis and Waawaatesi, must have called her to give her the news. I remember her and a white man, presumably one of her boyfriends, pulling into the driveway in a new car, stepping out into our muddy yard all dolled up in expensive clothes, not a hair out of place, too much makeup, fake eyelashes, bright red lipstick, fur coat, chinchilla, she would tell me later.

"Carolina," she said when she came in the door, making a grand entrance. She walked across the room, bent down where I was sitting, the strong smell of her perfume, and gave me a kiss on the cheek. "I'm so sorry about Bill."

She was there less than an hour, sitting next to me, clinging tightly to her purse, talking a bit too loud, mostly about herself, occasionally looking down her nose around the room at the others gathered there, making me wonder if maybe she had a drink or two on her way up from Duluth. She refused all offers of coffee, sweets or any of the dozens of casseroles.

"Oh, no," she said. "We're going to dinner at a supper club in Grand Rapids on our way back to Duluth."

She never took the time to go near the casket, or put *asemaa* in the mourning fire. Our conversation, or to be more accurate, her talking, all in English. I accidently responded to her once in our language and she gave me the deer in the headlights look of someone who didn't understand a word of what I was saying.

When she stood to leave, I noticed her perfectly manicured fingernails. I'm sure they were glue-on.

"If you ever find your way to Duluth, I hope you stop by for a visit," she said. Then she was off.

My sister, reluctantly Ojibwe.

Her friend, or whatever he was, standing silently beside her all the while they were there, an awkward, sheepish grin on his face, hands neatly folded in front of him, looking like he worked for a funeral home. I'm sure he had never been in a room filled with reservation Indians before, and never would again, obviously looking and feeling completely out of place.

⋲━━►━━╼ ⋅

I lived alone in our house in Pennington until 2008, when I retired at the age of 65. After Bill's passing, I put my energy into Andonis and Waawaatesi, their children, my grandchildren, work, crafts, powwowing, the lodge. I kept myself busy. Andonis had moved to the Twin

Cities after college for work. She married a Dakota man and had three children. They would come north on holidays and occasionally in summers to visit me, their *Nookoo*, shortened Ojibwe for *Nokoomis*, grandmother. My daughter Waawaatesi married a Cass Laker as soon as she completed her social work degree, had one child, a boy. They visited me all the time when I lived there. My grandson still calls me every week, he now a grown man, working out in Rapid City for a Native run foundation.

I would sing to my grandbabies when they were young, in the language. They learned all my favorites. I hope when they become someone's *mishomis*, grandfather, or *nokoomis*, grandmother, they teach the songs to them. One of my favorites.

> *Asabikeshiihn gii-akwaandawe*
>> The little bitty spider did climb up
> *Gii-gimiwan gaa-izhi-bangishing*
>> It did rain and she went down
> *Giizis ogii-baasaan gakina nibi*
>> The sun came out and dried up all the water
> *Miinawaa asabikeshiihn neyaab gii-akwaandawe*
>> And the little bitty spider went back to climbing up[8]

Through the years I've helped license many Native people to be foster and adoptive parents for our Native children. If I have a legacy, maybe that is what it will be, knowing the little boys and girls I've placed into care will be raised in Native homes, close to their communities, surrounded by the love and support of our people. That is the way it was done for generations by our ancestors. We again have accepted the responsibility of caring for our own.

I remain active in the lodge, camp out in the bush three seasons a year during ceremonies, work with the young girls who attend and new initiates. In winter, I stay in a nearby hotel come ceremony time. Now the elder, I am the one who talks story into the early morning hours each night there in the teaching lodge. And all while talking story, working with our hands, beading, sewing, doing quillwork, working birchbark, making outfits, moccasins. Always in the language, then translating it into English for the ones who are just learning to speak *Ojibwemowin*. I still go to all the powwows throughout Minnesota and Northwestern Wisconsin, dancing, selling my crafts. I still think I can dance up a storm, nearly as well as I did thirty years ago, get just dusty out there in the powwow arena.

Holaay . . . that's Native for surprising oneself.

<hr>

One morning a few years after I retired, the phone rang about fifteen times. I was outside pulling weeds in one of the flower beds, forgetting to take the phone with me wherever I went. Slammed the screen door on my way in the house, answered the phone huffing and puffing.

"Yah?" I said, nearly out of breath. A hesitant voice on the other end.

"Carolina? It's June."

My sister, who I hadn't heard from since Bill's funeral years ago.

She talked on and on, mostly about herself, for the longest time. Me, wondering why she had suddenly become my sister again. Wondering if she was ever going to tell me what she wanted, why she called in the first place.

Finally.

"Carolina, do you ever think you might move closer to me? I miss you so much, sister. Maybe you would even move in with me? We could take care of each other. I have a small, mother-in-law apartment on the first floor of my place. It needs a lot of work, but it has a wonderful view of the city. Maybe you could come down and take a look at it, and we could visit and talk about it?"

I, wondering if this was really my sister on the other end of the line. And if it was, wondering if something was wrong, if she was having some kind of neurotic episode.

Anyway, she went on and on for almost another hour, until I didn't have any feeling in the ear that was next to the phone.

"Come down, okay?" She said, just before she finally hung up.

"I love you, Sister," she said, hanging up.

What in the world, I was thinking.

I thought about that phone call for days afterwards. June and I had never really gotten along as children. Most of our adult lives she went missing, avoiding any family contact. She was barely present at our parent's funerals, leaving as soon as they were over, slipping out without saying so much as a goodbye.

Now, all of a sudden, she was there on the other end of the phone line, inviting me to come live with her?

Her call, however, gave me cause to think. I was living in a three-bedroom rez house out in the bush all my myself. It was paid-off, but the utilities were draining on me. As a social worker I hadn't made a lot in terms of wages, and that translates into not much social security retirement payments. Certainly, I had enough to get by, just barely. I had my side gig, making and selling crafts, but that was limited to summer powwow season. Fuel and electric bills never go down, only up higher and higher. Food costs were high as well, although I often ate during weekdays at Elderly Nutrition in the elder complex in Cass Lake. My roof was going to need replacement in a couple of years. The furnace was twenty years old. I didn't have any reserves to replace them when the time came.

I sat on her invitation for a month or more. Then, one day, I dialed her up and asked her if it would be okay if I drove down to Duluth for a visit.

"Oh, my favorite sister!" She, ecstatic. Me, thinking, my only sister.

So, I drove on down to Duluth a week later and made my way to her house, using the GPS on my phone to find her place. When I pulled into her driveway, I noticed the beautiful view. The whole city of Duluth and Lake Superior spread out before me, high on a hill over six hundred feet above downtown, docks, and warehouses, the city of Superior, Wisconsin across the bay.

We had a nice visit. I stayed for two days. She liked to talk about herself, of course. My warning bells should have been ringing out of control, but I didn't hear them if they were. She talked and talked. She had never been married. Could never find the right man, she said. Never had children. Never wanted children.

She said she like to travel, and had plenty of girlfriends she enjoyed visiting with, having fun with. I, probably much too settled for her taste. She, so obviously superficial, self-absorbed, probably hedonistic, fun, fun, fun.

We drove to the whole foods coop in her Subaru for all our meals while I was there. She didn't cook. Bought the organically-grown five-dollar coffees from the specialty drive-throughs. Her part of the house, upstairs, a large deck over-looking the city, impeccable. Big screen television, surround sound, cappuccino machine. The downstairs apartment where she wanted me to live, looking more a crack den.

"We'll fix it up," she said upon giving me the nickel tour.

I slept on her couch while I was there. Wondering if I had the energy to make the downstairs my own.

I, thinking on the drive back to Cass Lake that I would try it. Make the move. Become a big city girl. I'd lived my whole life on the reservation, out in the bush. Now alone for many years, I didn't see that changing. If I stayed, I'd probably die alone in my house. And when I died my cats, if I had any, would get hungry from me not feeding them, and eat me.

The reservation bought my house. I gave most of the money earned from the sale to my daughters, kept some to remodel the first-floor apartment in Duluth. To save money, I did much of the work as I could myself. Patched, scraped, painted. Had a flooring company from Cloquet come in and put in new carpeting. Hired someone to refinish the kitchen cabinets, someone else to gut and completely remodel the bathroom, put new windows in, fixed a broken garage door, resided the garage, reroofed it, planted flowers to replace the weeds that surrounded the yard. Bought bargain sale furniture and a small television, replaced the hot water heater, put in a gas fireplace, a new refrigerator, stove.

All told, I spent over forty-thousand dollars fixing the place up. That and paying my sister three hundred dollars a month, my share of the utilities.

Meantime, my sister, living above me, beyond her means. Running up her credit cards buying things she couldn't afford, flying off to Florida, Las Vegas with her girlfriends. Having parties, flavor of the month boyfriends, all older white men. Coming down to borrow from me on a regular basis. Money to help pay the real estate taxes, gas bill, to get the Subaru fixed.

Then one day, a boyfriend moves in with her. He looks married. I don't know, I guess married men have that look. He doesn't have a real first or last name. Goes by the name Dutch. Talks loudly, says ignorant things, cuts down Mexicans, Blacks. Makes contorted faces when telling inappropriate jokes about people with disabilities. My sister, laughs, thinks it's funny.

They are both driving me crazy.

Then, one day, his Cadillac Escalade is missing from the driveway and she comes down to see me.

"Dutch is moving in with me," she says. "We're thinking we'd like to have the place to ourselves. Do you think you could find your own place?"

I, of course, wanting to strangle her right there. Instead, got all *mindaway*, so mad my lower lip quivers and I can't respond.

Anyway, that's how I ended up living in my little apartment a couple blocks up from the Indian center near downtown Duluth. In the process, I lost all the money I put into remodeling the apartment my sister had invited me to move into. She never paid me back a dollar of what she borrowed from me.

Andonis, Waawaatesi, and their husbands came to Duluth and helped me move out when the day came. I had told them everything June had done to me.

"Auntie's a bitch," Andonis said.

I seconded that.

A few months after I moved, I found out via moccasin telegraph that things with Escalade Man didn't work out as June had planned. Apparently, she began draining his bank account as well. He moved out, and she had to rent the downstairs out to traveling nurses.

She called me a few weeks after the boyfriend left her, most probably to go back to his wife. Said she regretted asking me to leave. Wanted to meet her at one of those expensive coffee shops to talk.

"*Gaween*," I said. No way.

She persisted, of course. And me, I guess I'm a sucker, one of the many that are born every day. I've done my best to forgive her. I guess I've done that, for the most part. I'll never, ever, however, trust her again. She'll always be a con. She is, however, my only sister, the one who has never apologized for her betrayal, never paid a nickel back of what she owes me.

Eventually, and it took a few years, I took her back into my life. She's grown up a bit, I think, mellowed. Now she's gone full blown Ojibwe on us, attending language table at the Indian center, making a dance outfit, wearing all kinds of turquoise, beaded earrings, correcting people when they say an Ojibwe word incorrectly, going to women's sweats, thinking she knows more than anyone about our culture and history. We started traveling the powwow trail together. I still camp out near the powwow grounds. She stays in the nearby casino hotels. I eat the fry bread tacos they sell at the food vendor booths. She eats at the seafood buffets at the casinos. I do most of my clothes shopping at the charity shops. She buys her clothes at the used boutique stores. If she had the money, she would frequent the upscale clothing stores. My sister June still sometimes shows the cowgirl in her though, wearing a ratty cowboy hat and boots whenever we head down the road to the next powwow. Dyes her hair, black, of course.

Andonis says she's still a bitch.

I went all Native decorating my apartment. A Pendleton blanket covering a fading old couch, photos of Bill and I, our daughters, all in dance outfits, hanging on the walls next to pictures of Sitting Bull, Chief Buffalo. Braided sweetgrass, sage carefully dangling from the pictures. An abalone shell, filled with cedar, sitting on the coffee table, star quilt on my bed, gifted to me at Lower Sioux when I won the lady's traditional dance category some years back. A printed copy of the next season's powwow schedule on my refrigerator door, held in place by a magnet I got from Black Bear Casino down the road near Carlton on the Fond du Lac Reservation.

The year was 2015. I, now seventy-two years young. Hair long gone grey, beginning to stoop when I walk, just a bit. Blame it on the hills in Duluth. Worrying about climbing up and down stairs, falling, breaking a hip, pelvic bone, losing the ability to take care of myself, dementia, Alzheimer's disease. My crafts taking me longer to make. Threading beading needles taking me forever, the beads seem smaller, poking myself with the porcupine quills I use, moosehide and birchbark tougher to punch through. The trips out in the bush to get my medicines take longer, I, walking slower. Kneeling down to gather my medicines, I sometimes worry about being able to get up, getting lost in the bush, tripping over a stump. My knees sometimes lock.

This getting old isn't for sissies.

I, spending much of my time alone, watching too much television, Netflix, Prime. Getting hooked on series shows, living on ramen, bologna sandwiches, not caring to cook anymore. Ordering things from Amazon I didn't need. Realizing I need to get out and get moving. That is when I started my volunteer work. That's how I found my way to the women's shelter and hospital. I needed to do more, give back more.

January began cold, stayed that way. My night to volunteer at the hospital, just eight or so blocks down the way. I bundled up to keep warm, put a hand-knitted scarf over a tossle cap for double measure. Made my way down my stairs, then through the alley and onto the street, the snow crunching beneath my feet.

I made it to the hospital, signed in, asked the duty nurse where I was needed. She said there's a code blue, a Native man coming in by ambulance from Cloquet, down the freeway some twenty miles. They didn't know the particulars.

My world changed then, forever.

I found your poetry in the tattered book you carried deep inside your knapsack when they brought you into hospital. We had to dig through your things to find out who you were. There with your flute, a change of clothes. There all of your worldly possessions. And although I knew better, that I should not have violated your privacy, some inner voice called me to take your writings with me to the hospital chapel because I knew it would be empty and quiet. There I opened it and read each poem, each word singing, low and painful of deep longing and of loneliness. I heard your voice in each one, every word, pause, cadence. Each stood out to me in a different way, but one I read again and again, because it brought me back to that place from deep in memory, of the two of us when we were young, there at the cleave of the field behind the sister school.

There where we fell in love.

A Song Remembered

> Now an old man
> Sometimes I
> close my eyes
> and shut out the world around me
> and imagine you
> an old woman
> there in the circle of the dance area
> there
> wearing an old time black, floral beaded dress with
> moosehide moccasins
> dancing woodland style
> dancing there
> all by yourself
> and me
> singing a song remembered
> by only the oldest of grandmothers sitting under the arbor
> in the elder area
> and then
> I see on your face
> a recognition
> you, remembering the time
> I sang the song for you
> long ago
> when we were children
> there
> in a field of buttercups and sage and red clover
> behind the girl's dorm
> at the sister school
> and just then
> in my imagining
> you look my way
> and see the young boy you once loved
> as I sing for you

Simon

Carolina

One of the nurses in emergency asked if I knew him. I couldn't find words, hesitant, afraid to open my mouth should my emotions get the better of me. What would I say? That I knew him a lifetime ago? That we met at the sister school, the place nuns and a priest tried their best to strip us of everything that was Native? That he rescued me from there, made sure I safely made it home after being raped by the priest? That he was my first love?

I, eyes facing down toward the floor, nodded to her, indicating that I, indeed, knew him.

"Do you know if he has family? We'll need to contact them," she asked.

I shook my head, indicating that I did not.

I had just come from the hospital chapel, where I had been sitting for an hour or more. There, a statue of Jesus hanging on the cross. And there, just off to his right, one of his mother Mary, kneeling in prayer before him. On the other side, an angel of the Lord, as they call him, eyes looking lovingly up toward Jesus, the heavens. I, no Christian, knowing little about their ways except what I had learned when attending weddings and funerals of friends and acquaintances over the years. I, sitting there in one of the back pews, hands clinging to the book of Simon's writings, eyes looking up toward the front cornice of the room, that place where the wall and ceiling meet. Looking up, praying to my Creator for him, Simon. I, asking Simon, where had he been all these many years? He, down the hall behind closed doors, emergency, a team of doctors and nurses hovering over him, doing their best to keep him breathing, alive.

And me, there.

Memories of the sister school flooding through me. Of times huddled with other Ojibwe girls on the backside of the church after Sunday mass, there in our uniforms and closely cropped hair, there talking of things, holy water, acts of contrition, water and wine, the blood of Jesus, Hail Mary, the Lord's Prayer. Huddled, whispering, sharing in our language what we had told the priest in the confessional. Some, confused, raised in ceremonies, believing the words of the nuns, that the Catholic way was the only way, that our Creator was a false god. Pharisees, blasphemy, words intended to change young minds. Some of the doubters later baptized, seeking redemption, kneeling by their bedsides saying the prayers of their rosaries late in the evenings in the girl's dorm. Me, raised strong in our ways, telling the doubters that there are many paths to the Truth, that our Creator is the same one they speak of.

Memories of the times I would walk with some other girls down the trail out behind the school yard to the edge of the school cemetery, surrounded by a white picket fence in need of paint, repair. Fenced to keep their spirits there, confined so they could not escape to tell their stories. All the little crosses, angled this way and that. Grass grown tall, nourished by the dead.

We, the living, standing just outside the cemetery, forbidden to enter the space by the nuns, priest. Picking the petals from the fall flowers, scattering them into the wind over the fence. Knowing the children buried there were the ones who came before us, who came there in horse-drawn wagons and by steam train, our great grandmothers and great grandfathers, their sisters, brothers, aunties, uncles. Buried there, far from families, home, ceremony, never sent off on their spirit journey the proper way. Their spirits still there, waiting.

Waiting for someone to bring them home.

———————

The evening he arrived at hospital I asked the duty nurse if I might use my time that night in the laundry, kitchen, instead of visiting with patients. Folding towels, pillow cases, sheets, putting the spoons in their proper places. In the laundry, distracted from what was going on in emergency by the noises of hospital grade washers, dryers, all linen carefully-sanitized, steam ironed. Careful attention to ensure no germs, pathogens survived the process. Then to the kitchen, where I was given responsibility of ensuring silverware was put back into its proper places, lined up straight. All thoroughly clean, sanitized. Me there, dressed in a gown, hair covered, scrubbed in, a surgeon of the kitchen.

All evening there, having lost track of time. I should have signed out at midnight, walked through the cold back to my apartment, gone to bed with my headphones on, floated off to sleep listening to Mel Torme'.

Finally, another duty nurse, the other long gone home, telling me it was time to leave. "You look tired, Grandma Carolina," she said. "You need to go home and get some sleep."

On my way out, stopping by emergency, inquiring to the nurses at the front desk.

"That Native man that was brought in last evening," I asked. "Can you tell me about him, his condition?"

Me standing there leaning over the counter, volunteer identification card dangling around my neck, the photo on it, that of an elderly woman looking much older than the real me, or so I thought.

One of the nurses, young and perky, looks me over up and down.

"Are you family?"

Just in time, a nurse who knows me, always calls me her grandmother, intervenes.

"You mean Simon Pendagayosh, don't you?"

I nod.

"Mr. Pendagayosh is in ICU. To be honest, he is very ill. He has severe frostbite. We're not sure he is going to make it through this."

I take the elevator down to ground level, walk out into cold so extreme I have to catch my breath, cover my mouth with my free hand even though it is hidden by a scarf. I walk home, climb the steps to my apartment, careful not to slip, put the key in the door and push it with my shoulder knowing it often freezes shut, and go in.

There, making a pot of strong coffee, a piece of toast for breakfast. And there on the kitchen counter, sitting all dusty and alone, the cappuccino machine I took from my sister's place before I was forced to move out, taken without her knowledge as partial repayment of what she owed me. There, unused since the day I became its new owner. I, remembering asking her once, "What is this cappuccino anyway?"

My sister, looking long down her nose at me.

"You just to need to try it, Carolina. You'll never have plain old coffee again."

I just might do that someday. I have the machine to make it.

Finally, lying down to take a nap, wrapped in my Pendleton blanket, my head buried in a new therapeutic pillow I was just breaking in, bought at TJ Max as a Christmas present for myself. Eventually falling into a fitful sleep, not waking until just before noon, slobber on my new pillow, all tangled up in the blanket.

Sitting there in my recliner all afternoon, football on the television, the Packers and Vikings. The Vikings losing big. They always do. I don't even ever watch football.

Memories of Simon.

Of him telling me about his family walking up the road to his reservation church in winter, his mother and father, sisters, brothers. Their names I don't remember, but I imagine them, the way they look, their mannerisms.

Simon used to make me laugh sometimes, telling me about them.

"My mother," he had said. "She has these long, skinny brown fingers, and when I did something wrong, she'll point right at me and tell me to knock it off."

He would stick out his pointer, brown and not so skinny, right between my eyes, mimicking his mother's voice. I would stick out my lower lip, the way the old time Ojibwe do, and mimic my mother's voice, slow and soft and low in broken English.

"You kits behave yourselves. I'll get your dad!"

And we would laugh.

Then he would tell me about running dogs with his father, and although I had never even seen a team of sled dogs, imagined it as he talked story. Simon, a master of words, details. So precise in his description it was almost like I was there, sitting in the sled as it made its way down the trails, the dogs panting, vapor rising with each breath. My cheeks, eyeballs even, freezing from the cold. Then he would tell of when they would return home, of hanging the halters and gang lines in their proper places, propping the sled up against a shed wall, leading the dogs one by one to their pen. Then of them entering to their house, frost on their eyebrows and just below their noses, taking off their hats and coats and hanging them on the nails protruding from the side of a kitchen wall, removing wet choppers and boots and setting them next to the wood stove to dry. Then of his father pouring them each large cups of coffee, *makaday muskiki waboo*, black medicine water, some powdered milk, heaping tablespoons of sugar, and then, sitting at the kitchen table talking story to his wife, Simon's mother, about the dogs, the run.

Simon and me, out there on a park bench in Granite Falls, hidden among the trees so no one would discover us on the Saturdays we were allowed to go to town. Hiding from the priest. Or Simon and me, sitting in the grass in the field behind the girl's dorm at the sister school, talking story, in whispers.

Remembering when he took me safely home after what the priest did to me. Of my torn dress, blood on the floor there in the sacristy of the church. Of walking for miles down the dusty road leading from the sister school, sleeping huddled together under trees surrounded by corn fields. Of walking more, making our way using side streets, around Granite Falls, jumping in ditches and behind whatever there was to hide behind whenever a car came along. Of the Native family who picked us up and drove us to a bus station, fed us fry bread. Made sure we had enough money for me to make it home. Of Simon and me, my head resting on his shoulder as we made our way north on the bus. Of walking through the darkness all night until dawn, to home.

Of him telling me, against my will, that he must leave me there. Of him walking away down the road, me left standing there at the end of my family's driveway. Of how he stopped, turned, and waved to me before he disappeared around a corner.

Of how I sat there in the middle of the driveway crying for an hour or more, finally forcing myself to stand and make the slow walk to my home.

Of never seeing him again. Of always wondering about him. Simon.

———✒———

Now an old lady, living alone. Still on rare occasions the nightmares about the priest all those years ago, the matron leading me to him. She, who reminded me of my aunties. She, the one who led me there like a lamb to slaughter.

No one to awaken, comfort me now.

I returned to hospital that evening, signed in, checked with the duty nurse.

"Carolina, we're not expecting you until next weekend."

I made something up. Told her I was bored at home, that I'm not into football. I learned to lie at the sister school.

I did my rounds, visited the children and their parents, when they are there. Read to the ones who found themselves alone in their rooms, or with other children with whom they shared a room. Went from room to room doing the same.

"Any elders I should visit?" I asked the duty nurse when I was done with the children.

She directed me down the hall to several elderly patients, both lying there in deep sleep, one whose breathing was in the death rattle. There alone to die. I stayed with him the longest, prayed for him. Asked my Creator to take his hand, lead him down that final, earthly path, the one we, the living, are not yet ready to tread.

A nurse entering quietly on occasion, checking his pulse, monitoring his vital signs. We exchanged glances. She smiled slightly at me. I nodded in return. Me, sitting there beside him, watching the monitors. His breathing slowing, long and shallow.

I, having done this too many times to count. Sat there for several hours. I knew when it was his time. Soon, taking his hand and covering it with both of mine, praying under my breath to my Creator. Then he was gone.

After locating the nurse, I checked in again at the nurse's station, asking if there was anyone else for me to visit, sit with. She told me she didn't think so, that I may as well sign out and go home. On my way I walked long hallways to the east elevators, made my way up to ICU, checking in at the duty station.

"Do you have a patient here, Simon Pendagayosh?" I asked.

"Are you family?" A nurse asked.

"Yes, he is my cousin," I lied. Well, maybe just a small lie. We Ojibwe all seem to be cousins sometimes.

"Let me see," she said, opening a file on her computer, her fingers moving madly to retrieve the information I was seeking. Finally, her eyes looked at the screen, then up at me, reading to me.

"When Mr. Pendagayosh was brought to us his skin was white, blue, and blotchy, and the tissue underneath was hard and cold to the touch. There was damage beneath his skin to some of his tendons, muscles, nerves, and bones. He has deep frostbite. We don't know how long he was out in the cold before a driver going by noticed him lying there on the sidewalk. When he arrived here at the hospital, his pulse had slowed significantly, his body temperature was way down. He required urgent medical attention. The doctors and nurses in ER did what they could to stabilize him. They worked most of the first night just to keep him with us.

Simon has third stage frostbite. At a minimum, the lower layers of the skin of his hands, feet, ears, and nose, froze. He has large blisters on the frostbitten skin. His frostbitten skin will most probably turn black because the skin cells die after freezing. We have him on strong pain medication and are keeping him sedated. He is intubated. We're monitoring his condition often. We don't know if he is going to need surgery eventually to remove the carapace, the skin that was so badly damaged. We don't know the extent of damage to the internal tissues or bones. I can say that he is very ill. It could go either way for him.

"I'm sorry. Because of the extent of his injuries, he is being isolated."

I thanked her for the update, left for home. Over the next few days, I called ICU to check regularly about his condition. They kept me updated.

He had been given Loprost, a medication used to treat severe frostbite, which works by widening the blood vessels that supply blood to the affected body parts. This was because the damage was threatening to cause the loss of limbs, fingers, toes. That if some of the tissues of the affected body parts were to die (gangrene), they would need to be removed. The procedure to remove dead tissue the nurse referred to as debridement. There was a possibility he could lose his fingers, toes, that they may need to be removed.

"He is being kept in isolation," she said. "There are no visitors allowed at this time. We'll closely monitor his condition over the next several weeks."

My weekend evening to volunteer came again at the hospital. I signed in, did my rounds.

"Grandma Carolina!" The children who are there long-term said to welcome me when I entered their rooms. I had carefully selected what I might read to them based on their interests, as best I could. Sometimes stopping at a used book store, or Dollar Tree, to buy children's stories for my own collection, to read to children there in hospital.

I had several new elders to visit, one who was Native, her diabetes out of control. Family was there that evening, husband, children, grandchildren. One of them had stopped at KFC for chicken, bought a bucket, some rolls, honey packets. The patient lying in bed, ill, yet still smiling. Everyone there in the room, it smelling of chicken. All Ojibwe as can be.

I stopped and poked my head inside the room.

"*Aniin, boozhoo,*" Hello.

"*Aniin, boozhoo,* Auntie." One of the young ones replied back to me.

I waved, continued on my way. Down the hall to the room of an elderly white lady. I poked my head into the room.

"Hi there," I said. "Would you like some company?"

She welcomed me in. Talked my ear off. Told me she had knee surgery that morning.

"I'll be able to dance again," she laughed groggily.

She and her husband worked a farm down the freeway out of Mahtowa, some forty miles south of Duluth. Said she's been married to the same man for nearly fifty years. That they had raised dairy cows for years, but that dairying had long ago become a losing proposition. Now they lease most of their land out for haying. That their kids all left for cities, had no interest in carrying on farming.

"You're Native, aren't you?" she asked me.

"I'm about as Ojibwe as you can be," I replied, chuckling.

"We go to that Indian Black Bear Casino most every Saturday evenings," she said, "for the drawings and buffet. That's where our social security ends up."

"Me too," I say, laughing. The casinos, I'm thinking.

Our way of getting even.

<hr>

The next week I was on my way again to the hospital, shuffling slowly through fresh snow, careful not to fall, break a hip, end up in nursing care. I entered through the main door, said hello to the lady at reception, another volunteer, my boots wet from melting snow, rubber soles squeaking loudly as I made my way to the elevator. My sense of humor sometimes getting the better of me, wondering if squeaky boots understand what the other is saying.

I have a routine there, sign in, ask where I am needed, thinking maybe I'm becoming an institution. I did my rounds. My shift was supposed to end at midnight. I checked out a bit early that evening. Things were slow there.

So, I walked down the hall and took the elevator up to ICU, asked how Simon was doing. The nurse told me he was doing much better, that they would be moving him down to a regular room the next day. She said he'd be there for a few more days, then moved to a rehab center.

"When can I see him?" I asked.

"Tomorrow," she said. "Come back tomorrow after he has been moved."

Home again back to my apartment. Reruns. Jimmy Kimmel, Saturday Night Live, HGTV. I fell asleep in my chair, woke up with an urgent need to pee. Brushed the teeth that still called my mouth their home, made my way to bed. Laid there the rest of the night wide awake.

Sunday morning. Not planning on going to the hospital until the afternoon, when Simon would be moved down a few floors, able to accept visitors. Killing time, cleaning the appliances, the bathroom with vinegar and Dawn dishwash detergent mix. Shaking rugs, listening to Buddy Holly, Dion and the Belmonts, and Roy Orbison through my headphones. Trying to sing high to the song, "In Dreams," can't quite do it. The people downstairs must think there's an injured animal living above them.

Finally, lunch time. I made myself toasted cheese, tomato soup, tried not to spill any on my blouse. Took the rest of my pills. Put on makeup, blush, mascara, eyebrow pencil, lipstick. Chanel No. 5, earrings, a beaded barrette. Put on a dress, shoes in a bag for when I got to the hospital.

Looked in the full-length mirror that calls itself home on the back of my bedroom door. Not bad for an old lady, I was thinking. There was a time, long ago, when I turned many a head.

When I got to reception, I took off my boots and put on shoes, asked which room Simon Pendagayosh had been moved to. I took a deep breath, made my way to the elevator, popped Chiclets in my mouth. Up I went to the sixth floor. The elevator door took its time, finally opened. I stepped out, studying the room directory, arrows pointing this way and that. Down the hall, shoes clicking loudly, terrazzo floors. Finally, I was there, room 605.

I walked by, slowly, pretending I was a stranger, there to visit someone else. The room, filled with older Natives, most with grey hair, balding men, or men with caps on, wearing flannel, women in Pendleton coats. They were all talking to him. I couldn't see his face, too many arms, elbows, backs, bellies blocking my view. His family, I presumed. So, I walked by. Pretended I was going somewhere else. Made it to the end of the hallway, turned around, walked past them again, feeling like a stalker, back to the elevator, whistling softly to myself as I go. When I get nervous, I sometimes whistle.

The elevator arrived and I stepped inside, alone. My emotions, the anticipation of finally getting to see Simon after all the years, getting the better of me. Crying softly now, I can't seem to make it stop. I pushed the elevator button for the fourth floor, the wing I usually cover. When the door opened, I made my way quickly to the women's bathroom. I knew it well, went inside, found myself the only one there. There, I entered a stall in the farthest corner, hands covering my face, sobbing.

In time I was able to make the tears stop. I did my best to tidy myself, face flushed, eyes red and puffy. Then, making my way back to the elevator, I went to the cafeteria to kill time. There I drank two cups of coffee beyond my daily limit, until my hands were shaky, had a piece of lemon meringue pie. Looked at my watch at least one hundred times. Stared out the window at the ice on Lake Superior. One-hour passed, then another.

Finally, my courage built up again, a sugar high, I made my way up to the sixth floor again. Nearing his room, I listened for Native voices, the way we speak in that sing-song English.

Hearing none, I walked in. The room dark. Lying there, his hands and feet wrapped in bandages. I see he is still awake.

My throat dry, sounding as if I hadn't spoken in ages. I whispered. "Simon?"

CHAPTER THIRTEEN

The Bush

Carolina

I saw an old man lying in the hospital bed, pale, although his hair was still dark like I remembered, only now with streaks of grey, thinning, eyes hollow and sickly. He looked up at me the longest time, studying my features, thinking back long in memory. The two of us, speaking the language of silence.

I bent down closer to him, closer so he could hear me, whispered to him in our language.

"Simon, do you remember me?"

His eyes moving back and forth, studying me. Then, slowly, he raised an arm, the one not hooked to an IV, his bandaged hand touching my cheek. His voice, rough, injured from too long intubated, not yet healed.

"Carolina."

He would tell me later that seeing me again after all the years was like remembering an old song that would play over and over again in his head, one sung to, listened to long into the night.

We visited just a short while that evening. I could see he was weak, his body traumatized by what it had been subjected to. I did most all the talking. A quiet one, he, just as I remembered, yet still showing his sense of humor, turning his head, pointing out the window of the room with his bandaged hand.

"They gave me a room with a pretty good view."

The lights of the hillside, the city of Duluth, there out the window. I, moving toward the window myself, pointing.

"My place is just down that way a few blocks."

Small talk. Neither of us knowing quite what to say.

"I was here earlier to see you. The room was filled with *neej's*, friends," I said.

"My family," he replied. "My sisters and brothers. Most I hadn't seen in years, except my sister Annie."

"They must have missed you a great deal," I returned.

I could see the look on his face of one who carries long ago regrets, the kind etched deep into the soul, residing there.

"Mmmn," he said. "I should have listened to myself more."

My hand touched his face.

"Simon, I'm going to go now, okay? Let you rest."

He nodded.

"Can I come see you again?"

He smiled up at me then. I hadn't seen that smile in nearly sixty years.

"Come here," he said, a twinkle hidden deep somewhere in his sad eyes. I, leaning in closer to him. Simon, kissing me on the cheek.

⟶

I went to see him nearly every day after that. Reminiscing about our times at the sister school, the Saturdays we would meet in the park in Granite Falls, evenings out in the field behind the girl's dorm. Sneaking glances on the bus, in the halls of the school, dining room, passing in the yard. The nuns. We laughed, made fun of them when we talked, mimicked them telling us to finish our oatmeal, sit up straight, sharpen our pencils, be quiet, pray. Especially, pray. Avoiding any talk of the priest. Simon, not sharing what he had done to Father Adrian, of his time spent in reformatory.

All of that would come later.

Eventually, he was moved to a rehab center for nearly a month to recover, heal. I got to meet one of his sisters there when we both showed up nearly the same time to visit him. Annie and I got along right away. She invited me out to the event center at the Black Bear Casino on Fond du Lac Rez for the Thirteen Moons Powwow. We got to visit while there, danced our tails off. We've become good friends, go to bingo at the casino together once in a while, rummaging on Fridays in Cloquet. Annie had just recently lost her husband. I could really relate to what she was going through. We've shared our secrets. I can tell she loves her brother a great deal, fusses over him, tells him to knock it off when he gets to teasing her, or me, too much.

"Just quit it, eh," she will say. Just rezzy sounding.

When Simon was in rehab, I had to have a sit-down with the director there because I noticed they weren't changing the linens on his bed enough, emptying the trash, cleaning his room, or helping him shower like they should. Aides, or whoever was supposed to be doing these things were sluffing off, I imagine, staring at their phones too much, texting. I never told Simon a thing about it. In my imagining, though, I sometimes wish he could have seen that little white man director, looking just scared when I was in his office, giving him a brow beating. You don't want to make a Native woman angry. Simon's room was clean the next time I went to visit him, sheets and pillow cases looked like they'd just been changed. Simon looked all scrubbed up as well.

He told me he loved me that day I went to visit him, that he has loved me since we first met that long ago Saturday on the street in Granite Falls, that our chance reunion was more than serendipity.

"*Gi-zaagi'in, niinimoshenh,* I love you, sweetheart."
We both said it at the same time.

Simon

When I came out of it in ICU, I had no idea where I was at first. Tubes hanging out of me all over this way and that, machines blinking and beeping, all bandaged up. Finally, a nurse came in and I asked him where I was, and he told me.

"Someone found you lying on a sidewalk on Fourteenth Street in Cloquet, covered with a dusting of snow. You must have fainted and when you fell, bumped your head. You're here for severe frostbite."

I'd never been hospitalized before, but probably should have been many times, given the life that I'd lived. I must have passed out from dehydration, not eating all day, getting little sleep the night before I got on the bus. I was completely out of it for nearly two weeks.

The doctor came in to see me the next day. Said I was very fortunate I wasn't going to lose any of my extremities, but that I'd need to spend some time in rehab once I got out of hospital. My family found out where I was. Annie had called my cell phone when I didn't show up at her place, but it went straight to voicemail. After a few hours, she said, she called the police. Luckily, by then someone had seen me, a lump in the middle of a sidewalk, and called 911.

That first afternoon they moved me out of ICU and into a regular room my brothers and sisters came to see me. I told them they'd all gotten old, except for me. My sister Annie must have guilted them all to come to visit me at the same time. I can't even describe the feeling of seeing them again after all those years.

After they left, I just lay there thinking how fortunate I was. Not just to be alive, but to be surrounded again in the loving circle of family. I hadn't realized how much I had missed that. Then, just as

I was getting groggy and almost ready to fall asleep, I heard a voice calling me. And I looked up and there was a woman standing over me, whispering. I didn't recognize her at first, but then, I noticed her eyes. Carolina had the most beautiful, almond eyes. I've never been a religious man, in fact, I abhorred the church after what happened all those years ago at the sister school. That evening, however, at hospital when I saw her face, it was like the Creator had come and put its loving hand on my shoulder, reminded me it had always been there for me, returned her to me. Then, her voice,

"Simon?"

Once I got out of rehab, I went to stay with my sister Annie. I still needed in home physical therapy. The doctor said I might always walk a bit wonky, but that I was fortunate to be able to walk at all. Sister and Carolina like to tease, use that physical humor we Native people thrive on, told me I walked a little like Frankenstein. Annie babied me, of course, found a way to hunt down some of the foods I hadn't eaten in years, catfish, rabbit, and tater tot hotdish made with ground moose meat.

My brothers and sisters came to visit me when I was staying at Annie's as well. She had a big feed to celebrate me returning home and invited all of them, their kids and grandkids, and Carolina. I met many of my nieces and nephews then, forgot most of their names before they even left that evening. Each of them seemed so kind and respectful to me, addressing me in a proper, respectful way as Uncle.

Carolina would drive from Duluth to see me every other day. We shared the paths our lives had taken. I told her what I had done to Father Adrian, about spending time in reformatory, all the years I'd spent living on and off the streets, that I probably should have been dead a long time ago the way I lived. Then I told of the incident about the death of the homeless mother and her two little babies that finally made me realize my life up until that time had gone nowhere, that I needed to sober up. I told her I had gotten a teaching job for nine years after that, of volunteering at a feeding center, of leaving food and smokes for the homeless that lived up and down Franklin Avenue.

"How long you been clean now?" She asked.

"Just over ten years," I said.

Carolina shared her story with me, about the different jobs she'd held, marriage, daughters, grandchildren. The path her life had taken so different than the one I had lived. As an adult she had never touched alcohol. It wasn't allowed in her home. She was a traditional woman, a dancer, healer, maker of crafts. one who held a significant role in her lodge. Carolina had always found ways of giving back, even in retirement, working with Native women, volunteering at hospital.

Our lives taking divergent paths, each of us making both conscious and unconscious decisions along the way, both affected by happenstance, circumstances, timing, luck, sometimes divine intervention, our lives going this way and that. We aged, now nearing the end of our circle here on *aki* and looking back, in wonderment of how quickly the time has passed, thinking in hindsight of some of the choices we have made, what we might have done differently.

Then we look ahead and there is just us, Carolina, Simon.

Annie let me borrow her car to move things out of my old apartment in Minneapolis. Most everything, the bed, dresser, some clothes, mismatched cookware and plates, bent spoons and forks, donated to the Salvation Army. I retrieved several boxes of my Native authored books, a partially completed flute I was working on. While I was there, I made my rounds to the feeding center where I had been volunteering, said goodbye to several street friends I knew, old drinking buddies. Before I left town, I swung by the Indian center to bid adieu to a few people I knew who had helped me with my recovery years back, and at the school where I had taught. The director there, Andonis, was at a hearing at the state capitol that day so I didn't get to see her.

I stayed with Annie for nearly five months. Spring came, mud season. Summer road construction began. Meantime, I began looking for my own place. I needed my own space where I could work on my writing, make a big mess with shavings and pieces of discarded wood carving flutes, bending the hoops of lacrosse sticks. Every other month, it seemed, in the rez newspaper, there would be a listing of homes that were reservation owned, having been rehabbed by the tribe's construction company, and were listed at a good price to be sold to tribal members at no interest via lottery drawings.

I applied for several of them. Competition was fierce. The winners were announced live on Facebook. One was a little cabin out in the bush on the south side of Big Lake, about ten miles west of the casino just off Highway 210. The day of the open house I had physical therapy so I missed it, but later on Carolina and I drove out and snooped around and looked it over, peeking in windows. Anyway, I was just walking into Annie's place late on the afternoon the day of the drawing and my phone rang, and it was the rez calling, informing me my name had been drawn. Me, the new owner of my own lottery dream home. I called Carolina as soon as I got off the phone, said we needed to celebrate, that I'd take her out to dinner.

When she came over that evening, we went down to the casino for the Mexican buffet.

Neither of us had a lot in terms of our retirement. We both had Social Security, Medicare, Indian Health Service to pay for what Medicare didn't cover. I had a nice monthly per capita payment from Fond du Lac Rez, courtesy of profits from our two casinos. The buffet was a special treat.

That evening after the buffet we stayed a while at the casino and played the slots, losing our mandatory five-dollar limit each. Sitting there, side by side, sipping on free root beer delivered via beverage cart. I just came out and asked her.

"Carolina, what would you think about moving in with me?"

I, having never lived with a woman before, never having been in a serious relationship before Carolina. Had, of course, my share of white girls when in university, later snagging one-night stands from the Indian bars in Minneapolis. Women who I woke up with in the morning, barely remembering their names. Women who would stay the night, a day, maybe two. My past experience with women reflecting an old saying we have about Native people and relationships. The saying goes that Native people don't date, they snag, and by the next day have moved in together and are calling each other, "babe."

"Hey, babe, get me a smoke, eh?"

Carolina and I, seen by most, I suppose, as a couple of old farts. Sitting there in the casino that evening, no more than six months after we had reunited after nearly sixty years.

"Sure," she said.

Carolina

We made a home together in our little lottery dream cottage out on the rez, moved all my stuff from my apartment in Duluth there so it's decorated all Native. I didn't hang the photo of Bill and I that we had taken at the powwow in Mille Lacs, of course. That went in the immigrant chest we bought at Goodwill in Duluth, along with all my old photos and keepsakes. I still dig it out, though, every once in a while. Love, you see, knows no bounds. I loved Bill very much. I've loved Simon most all of my life.

I probably started a trend. My sister June, I think, was a bit jealous when I told her I was moving in with Simon. Not that she had any interest in him. She would never be seen with a Native man. It wasn't more than a few months later when she announced a man was moving in with her, a white man, of course, her latest sugar daddy. Someone to add to her jewelry collection, take her on cruises, to his winter place in Sarasota. They come out to visit us every once in a while. He's okay, I guess, talks too much though, asks a lot of intrusive questions. I think we have a culture clash with white people like that sometimes. When white people get nervous, some of them start talking and won't shut up. When we Native people get nervous, we shut down. They are trying to be nice asking all their questions, make conversation. We Natives see it as intrusive, interfering. They are free with advice. We give advice sideways, talking story. The advice is always buried there in story. I don't know if we'll ever see eye to eye. We Natives who are raised Native don't even look others in the eyes.

It's complicated, I guess.

June will ride along with Simon and I sometimes when we go powwowing. Sits in the back seat, her hand mirror out, pulling chin hairs with a tweezers, admiring herself, making judgments about someone, something. I suppose I could just tell her we don't have any room, but I don't. I guess I sort of feel sorry for her, the way she is.

Andonis calls her the crabby auntie. We've all had at least one.

Simon comes out in the bush with me when I gather medicines. We use the little guest shed for drying, storing them, hang them from the rafters, in canning jars, spread out on benches, made into teas. Some we find right in our yard. Otherwise, we drive out to the ditch banks, a few miles away. He is learning to recognize them now as well, helps me spot them. My eyes aren't what they used to be. Then again, his hearing is going. The clinic got him a new set of hearing aids but he won't wear them. Said it was unmanly. I don't know about men sometimes.

We make and sell our crafts at community gatherings and powwows for extra spending money. People stop out at our cottage as well. Word got out quick that a couple of crafters moved on the rez. Actually, it's a pretty good side gig because we do cash sales only, don't have to report it to any government agency. In fact, we bought a newer car, a used Ford Taurus station wagon, with our craft money recently, sold my old one on Facebook Marketplace. Our new, old war pony for hitting the powwow trail.

Simon

Carolina kept her volunteer commitments. She drives into Duluth once a week to do her work at hospital and with the women's shelter. I found new places to give back here on the rez. I'm the official elder for the reservation lacrosse team. I don't coach or anything. My main job is to stand on the sidelines like a cheerleader. Of course, I say the opening and closing prayers before and after practices, teach the younger ones the fine art of stick making. I go to the recovery center once a week as well, say the opening prayer, play my flute when they gather in circle. I get invited to the tribal school to give lessons in stick making, making and playing the flute. I was drum hopping at the local powwows and the Spirit Mountain Singers asked me to join them, so I've found a home with a new group of singers.

I think as we get older, we've got to find ways to feel useful, keep busy. And we do that by giving back. Too many people just take. They spend their whole lives just taking up space. Then when it's nearly over, maybe they realize it. And they ask themselves, is that all there is?

I took up space for too many years. Now, it seems, I'm making up for lost time.

***

Late in the summer after we moved in together, Carolina and I took the long drive with our new war pony down to the powwow in Upper Sioux. We set up camp that Friday evening, walked the circle around the arena as crafters and food vendors were setting up, sat under the arbor of the elder area and listened to the drums during warmups.

I hadn't been down that way since we were there at the sister school as young people. It was on my mind, I guess, all those thoughts. So, I guess I just blurted it out loud.

"Carolina, what would you think of taking a drive up to the sister school tomorrow morning?"

I wasn't sure she would want to go there, that maybe it would just bring back bad memories of her days there, what happened there. She said she had come down to the Upper Sioux powwow for years, but had never had the nerve to take the short drive up to the school. Now, with me, she said she would go there.

We're early risers, up with sunrise. Made a pot of camp coffee, fired up the car and headed north.

I remember as we drove those last few miles on the dirt road leading to the school. Me, driving with one hand, the other resting on Carolina's shoulder.

Both quiet, speaking without mouthing words.

Finally arrived there. The remains of the school building, windows boarded and broken, grass grown tall all around, late summer flowers in all their pretty colors, blues, yellows, reds, whites. The old wooden dormitories long fallen into ruin, laying in a heap. The church and priest's residence completely gone, nunnery as well.

We walked in to take a closer look, not speaking a word to each other. Carolina took my hand. There to the place we had met on late evenings so many years ago.

There we settled into the tall grass at the cleave of the field and cottonwoods. Sitting near where the girl's dorm once stood of the sister school in a field of wildflowers and sage and red clover. Carolina in her ribbon dress, moccasins. There, we kissed, and when I turned my head away, thinking it would be on the cheek, she instead touched my face and turned me to meet my lips.

There, where we dreamed.

Carolina

After we sat in the field for a long time, we took a walk back to the car and got some *asemaa*, tobacco. Then out back of the school building through the long grass to the graves. The old picket fence, now gone, fallen, returning to dust, crosses strewn about. There at the edge of where the fence once was, we put our tobacco down, prayed quietly.

Standing there, it seemed I was just a young woman again, fourteen years old. Memories of the times I would walk with other girls down the trail out behind the school yard to the edge of the school cemetery, at that time surrounded by a white picket fence in need of paint, repair. Fenced to keep their spirits there, confined so they could not escape to tell their stories. All the little crosses, angled this way and that. Grass grown tall, nourished by the dead.

We, the living, standing just outside the cemetery, forbidden to enter the space by the nuns, priest. Picking the petals from the fall flowers, scattering them into the wind over the fence. Knowing those buried there were the ones who came before us, who came there in horse-drawn wagons and by steam train, our great grandmothers and great grandfathers, their sisters, brothers, aunties, uncles. Buried there, far from families, home, ceremony, never sent off on their spirit journey the proper way. Their spirits still there, waiting.

Still waiting for someone to bring them home.

<hr>

We returned to Upper Sioux powwow that afternoon just before grand entry. I dressed in my outfit quickly, got in line with the other elderly traditional female dancers. Simon, remaining there in the elder sitting area with the ribbon shirt on I had made for him. He'd dance a few inter-tribals with me later on. He didn't get out into the circle much because he said he looked a little too much like Frankenstein dancing. We Ojibwe like poking fun of ourselves as well.

That night after we returned to our tent and were sitting around the fire making smores he told me he'd had a visitor while sitting in the stands that day. That he'd borrowed money from him once, four dollars, finally paid him back. Jay, his old friend from the sister school, must have recognized him and came over and sat with him for a while.

"He asked me if I ever knew what happened to the priest, Father Adrian. I said I had no idea."

Jay said that two years after Simon and I had left the school, one of the nuns found Father Adrian's body in the creek out behind the field. He'd been beaten to death. The person or persons responsible were never caught.

"We all figured," Jay told him, "That it was some of the men from my community. They had gotten word of what he was doing to some of the girls there."

That old white man saying, "what goes around comes around." Karma, in Hinduism and Buddhism, the sum of a person's actions in this or past lives.

I slept like a log that night.

When the weekend was over, we packed up our things and pointed our dusty little station wagon north. Simon and I, the satellite radio in our car playing just loud.

Vince Gill.

Epilogue – The Elders

Traveling Song

Way hey ya hey ya hey oh

Way hey ya hey ya hey oh
Way hey ya hey ya hey oh

G'naadamoimin ina Gizhemanido?
Can you help us Great Spirit?
G'naadamoimin ina Gizhemanido?
Can you help us Great Spirit?
Gweyak ji bimoseyaang
To walk straight
Baa maampii g'ga waabamigom
So long and we will see yous

G'naadamoimin ina Gizhemanido?
Can you help us Great Spirit?

G'naadamoimin ina Gizhemanido?
　　Can you help us Great Spirit?
Gweyak ji bimoseyaang
　　To walk straight
Baa maampii g'ga waabamigo
　　So long and we will see you

G'naadamoimin ina Gizhemanido?
　　Can you help us Great Spirit?
G'naadamoimin ina Gizhemanido?
　　Can you help us Great Spirit?
Gweyak ji bimoseyaang
　　To walk straight
Baa maampii g'ga waabaminim
　　So long and I will see yous

G'naadamoimin ina Gizhemanido?
　　Can you help us Great Spirit?
G'naadamoimin ina Gizhemanido?
　　Can you help us Great Spirit?
Gweyak ji bimoseyaang
　　To walk straight
Baa maampii g'ga waabamin
　　So long and I will see you[9]

Andonis

I remember being up in Flambeau one time for some kind of gathering of tribal and charter school administrators at their hotel casino. It was early evening and I was bored, I suppose, having sat in meetings all day while representatives of the respective state education departments and Bureau of Indian Education talked funding, rules, and regulations. Me, drawing pictures of bears on the handouts, my *doodem*, clan.

So, after dinner I walked down a long hallway toward the slots and bingo hall. And when I was about to pass the bingo hall, I could see the games hadn't started yet. There, a small group of elderly Ojibwe women in the room, leaning forward toward each other, gathered in a circle. Curiosity got the better of me, so I walked, quietly, in toward them. And as I drew closer to them, I noticed the way they were speaking, lower lips pursed up the way our elderly women sometimes do.

They were whispering in the language.

Not wanting to intrude any more than I already had, I began to retreat, tiptoe backwards toward the door. One of them, however, must have noticed me there. She pointed up with her lips, motioning for me to come closer.

"I am so sorry," I said, in the language. "I just saw you all sitting there and it made me think of my mother and her cousins."

I had been thinking of my mother a lot that day, I don't know why. Remembering when I was young and she had her cousins over to visit, to drink tea, do their crafts. Me and my sister Waawaatesi sent off to play outside, and when the weather wasn't cooperating, to our room. I remembered all those times, my mother, her cousins, sitting there around the kitchen table, leaning in to get closer to each other, lips pursed, listening.

Speaking our language in whispers.

My mother called me at my work one morning, said she wanted my sister, Waawaatesi, and me to come up in a couple of days, that she had something she needed to talk with us about. She said to bring our husbands and their golf clubs. They could go play eighteen at the Bear in Carlton while we had our sit down. I called my sister as soon as my mother and I had said our *giga waabamin*, see you later, to ask her if she knew what was going on. She was, like me, clueless.

That day she sat in the middle of her sagging, faded couch in her Duluth apartment, and called us girls over to sit, one on each side of her. She held our hands. Then she was quiet for a long time, so quiet the only sound the hum of the refrigerator. Our mother, you see, sometimes speaks the language of silence. My sister and I both learned that language from our father and her. Then, finally, she spoke.

"I been wanting to tell you this story for a long time," she began.

She began by telling us how much she loved our father. How she wanted to ensure her story was not in any way meant to be disrespectful to his memory, of him.

"Mom," I said. I rested my head on her shoulder then, thinking of my father, how much I missed him. Looking over, I could see that Waawaatesi was in tears. She, the more sensitive of the two of us.

"My baby girls," she said. Both my sister and I nearly fifty years old.

So, she began, quietly speaking so we had to lean in closer to hear, listening and reading her lips as she spoke.

"His name is Simon," she began.

We, sitting there, as she told the whole story about the sister school, Simon, the priest. The field behind the girl's dorm, the park in Granite Falls where she would meet Simon. The matron, sacristy, what the priest had done to her. Of Simon ensuring she made it home safely, the years she wondered about him. Of how he ended up in reformatory for three years because of what he did to the priest.

The story went on for a long time. A mother, daughters, sitting there. And when she was done, she said funny things that made us laugh. I, noticing a bag of cheese puffs up on her kitchen counter, got up and retrieved them. Then the three of us, cheesy fingers and all, sitting on the couch, a mother and her daughters.

"Who is this Simon?" I asked.

She told us then. Simon Pendagayosh.

We live in such a small world.

"I know him!" I shouted. "Mother!"

Simon Pendagayosh had been my Ojibwe language teacher at Phillips Neighborhood Academy until he retired. I remembered back when he first came in for his interview, hair all slicked back, cleaned up, speaking that Fond du Lac dialect. And although I never shared this with him, I remembered him from the streets, Franklin Avenue. I used to see him there, for years, all messed up, hanging out on corners with other street people, bumming smokes and spare change. Sometimes as well at the Indian centers when he sobered up on occasion, there dressed in a baggy, stretched out sweater and pants he'd dug out the free boxes at one of the shelters.

Some months later our mother called us up again just after she and Simon moved in together into the lottery dream cottage he had won for cheap in a Fond du Lac reservation house drawing. I remember when we pulled into the driveway of their little cottage on Big Lake, out near Sawyer. My mother and Simon, sitting there on the porch, sipping on cappuccinos made from that machine she took from Auntie June. She, beading something for a new outfit for a granddaughter, one of my daughters. Simon, putting the final touches on a flute, a gift for Waawaatesi's husband.

"We're going to shack up," she said, first thing, laughing. Then continuing, "live in sin."

Holaay. That's Native for always being surprised when someone says something, well, surprising.

My mother could be so funny sometimes.

We brought a present for them that day, there in a box in the back seat, a female German Shepard puppy.

"Here's something to protect the two of you from them meth head home invaders," I said, teasingly. I remember telling Simon as I retrieved it from the back seat, cuddling it close to me as I approached them.

Simon took the pup and cuddled it close to his chest.

Waawaatesi asked, "Do you have a name in mind?"

"Oh yeah," he replied.

Vince Gill.

<hr>

One time when I was visiting my mother and Simon was out in their guest shed tinkering with something or the other, she showed me his writing. We sat there on their back porch while I read it page by page. I was so touched by it. Later, just before I left, I told Simon how much I loved what he wrote, his poems. A shy one, he, not saying a word, just smiling back at me.

A couple of months later I wrote a small writer's grant to the Minnesota State Arts Board to get a chapbook of Simon's works published. I, a decent grant writer, having to be one was part of my job as head of a school. Anyway, the grant was funded.

Simon polished up his work, added some fancy wording. We hired someone to do the graphic design and got a small print company in Duluth to print five hundred copies. The book sold just over four hundred copies and Simon got to do a book tour, signing and reading in several Duluth bookstores, the Indian center on second street, a Native-owned bookstore in the Twin Cities, and at Fond du Lac Tribal and Community College. I think he's really gotten to enjoy his fifteen seconds of fame. I went to his reading in Minneapolis. Simon, standing in front of a stack of his books, all scrubbed up, hair slicked back, dressed in a flannel shirt and jeans, all pressed by my mother. He cleans up good. My mother, sitting in a chair near him, beaming, just proud.

My mother and Simon, both in their eighties now. The last time we saw them my sister and I met up at Perkins in Cloquet for the senior special before we hopped in her car and headed out Big Lake Road, then down Maple Drive, to their little lottery dream cottage on the lake.

Vince Gill, an old lady herself now, bigger than hell, meeting us at the driveway, barking like mad. We, wondering if we should even get out the door, that she might bite one of our legs off.

My mother had just made a fresh pan of lug, so we sat out on their porch, picking little pieces off and eating away. We visited for a long time, talking back and forth in the language.

When it was time for us to leave, they both followed us around to the other side of the cottage, back to my sister's car.

I remember them now, clearly as if it was yesterday, my mother and Simon. Standing on the porch, holding hands, waving as we slowly backed out of the driveway.

Singing a traveling song.

Notes

1   narf.org/healing-from-boarding-school-policy-2/

2   gospelgo.com/n/ojibwe_hymns.htm

3   gospelgo.com/n/ojibwe_hymns.htm

4   gospelgo.com/n/ojibwe_hymns.htm

5   Ojibwe.net

6   Momaday, N. Scott. *The Gourd Dancer*. New York: Harper and
    Row, 1976.

7   Ojibwe.net

8   Ojibwe.net

9   Ojibwe.net

Acknowledgments

Through the years I've consciously tried writing different genre—poetry, prose, Ojibwe history and culture, academic research articles, educational textbooks, short fiction, and novels. I've always wanted to write a Native love story, so when Simon and Carolina appeared in my head and each began telling me their stories, I sat down and let it flow from them to my computer screen.

None of it would be possible without the assistance of others. I am indebted to them in developing the story. Marlene Wisuri, who saw promise in it and worthy of publication; my wife Betsy, who has read and edited every word of everything I write; Jay Peterson, who lent his name to the story; Ed Pfeiffer, who continues to provide many hours of financial advice and work without renumeration to our publishing efforts; Margaret Noodin, who generously consented the use of Ojibwe songs and prayers from Ojibwe.net.

About the Author

Thomas Peacock is co-publisher of Black Bears and Blueberries Publishing, specializing in Native books written by Native authors. He is a member of the Fond du Lac Band of Lake Superior *Anishinaabe Ojibwe* and lives with his wife Betsy on the Fond du Lac and Red Cliff Reservations. An invited speaker at numerous workshops, conferences, and community events, he received both his master's and doctoral degrees in educational leadership from Harvard University. He's been a teacher, secondary principal, superintendent, full professor, and associate dean in public and tribal schools, and universities. He was a Bush Leadership Fellow.

Of his numerous books published, *Ojibwe* and *The Good Path* were Minnesota Book Award winners. *The Seventh Generation* was multicultural children's book of the year (American Association of Multicultural Education). *The Forever Sky* received a Kirkus starred review (April 2019). *The Tao of Nookomis* and *Beginnings* were runner's up award winners at the Northeastern Minnesota Book awards. *The Wolf's Trail* (Holy! Cow Press) was Minnesota Library Association independent fiction winner for 2020 and One Book Northland in 2023. He has a forthcoming book, *The Naming of Aki*.